"Stay where you are!" Aaron's yell cut into the chaos like a knife. *"Nobody move!"*

Fragments of what was happening continued to tumble through Penelope's brain. People had escaped. But the window of opportunity had lasted less than a minute. Everybody left in the E.R. was now under the control of the gunman. It was a lottery that one of them might not survive the next few seconds.

"Do exactly as he says." Mark was watching Aaron as he spoke, and Penelope cringed. How could he draw attention to himself like that? He was inviting Aaron Jacobs to use him as a target and he was the closest person to the deranged patient other than herself.

The closest person who was alive, that was.

D0251601

Dear Reader,

Perhaps you are driving home one evening when you spot a rotating flashing light or hear a siren. Instantly, your pulse quickens—it's human nature. You can't help responding to these signals that there is an emergency somewhere close by.

Heartbeat, romances being published in North America for the first time, bring you the fast-paced kinds of stories that trigger responses to life-and-death situations. The heroes and heroines whose lives you will share in this exciting series of books devote themselves to helping others, to saving lives, to *caring*. And while they are devotedly doing what they do best, they manage to fall in love!

Since these books are largely set in the U.K., Australia and New Zealand, and mainly written by authors who reside in those countries, the medical terms originally used may be unfamiliar to North American readers. Because we wanted to ensure that you enjoyed these stories as thoroughly as possible, we've taken a few special measures. Within the stories themselves, we have substituted American terms for British ones we felt would be very unfamiliar to you. And we've also included in these books a short glossary of terms that we've left in the stories, so as not to disturb their authenticity, but that you might wonder about.

So prepare to feel your heart beat a little faster! You're about to experience love when life is on the line!

Yours sincerely,

Marsha Zinberg,
Executive Editor, Harlequin Books

EMERGENCY: CHRISTMAS

Alison Roberts

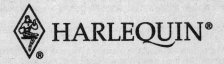

TORONTO • NEW YORK • LONDON
AMSTERDAM • PARIS • SYDNEY • HAMBURG
STOCKHOLM • ATHENS • TOKYO • MILAN • MADRID
PRAGUE • WARSAW • BUDAPEST • AUCKLAND

ISBN 0-373-51266-X

EMERGENCY: CHRISTMAS

First North American Publication 2003

Alison Roberts lives in Christchurch, New Zealand. She began her working career as a primary school teacher but now splits her available working hours between writing and active duty as an ambulance officer. Throwing in a large dose of parenting, housework, gardening and pet minding keeps life busy, and teenage daughter Becky is responsible for an increasing number of days spent on equestrian pursuits. Finding time for everything can be a challenge but the rewards make the effort more than worthwhile.

GLOSSARY

A and E—accident and emergency department

B and G—bloods and glucose

Consultant—an experienced specialist registrar who is the leader of a medical team; there can be a junior and senior consultant on a team

CVA—cerebrovascular accident

Duty registrar—the doctor on call

FBC—full blood count

Fixator—an external device, similar to a frame, for rigidly holding bones together while they heal

GA—general anesthetic

GCS—the Glasgow Coma Scale, used to determine a patient's level of consciousness

Houseman/house officer—British equivalent of a medical intern or clerk

MI—myocardial infarction

Obs—observations re: pulse, blood pressure, etc.

Registrar/specialist registrar—a doctor who is trained in a particular area of medicine

Resus—room or unit where a patient is taken for resuscitation after cardiac accident

Rostered—scheduled

Rota—rotation

RTA—road traffic accident

Senior House Officer (SHO)—British equivalent of a resident

Theatre—operating room

CHAPTER ONE

YES!

Penelope Baker was confident that her personal elation would be easily absorbed by the general buzz of anticipation building around her. She reached for the wall phone and punched in the required number to reach the operator.

'Could you page the anaesthetics registrar, please?' *Please!* Penelope added silently. Let Jeremy be on duty. Please, please, *please!*

She glanced over her shoulder as she waited, inner tension kicking in at the minor crisis erupting beside her. A student nurse, Chrissy, had been invited to join the trauma team for the incoming case and the poor girl was terrified. Having been directed to assist the circulation nurse, Chrissy was presently struggling to untangle the giving set she was attempting to prime. She had forgotten to close the line, and fluid was dribbling steadily from the end of the tubing. Droplets splashed Penelope as Chrissy shook the tubing to try and unravel the knot.

Behind Chrissy, the other team members appeared focused. Drugs were being removed from a secure cupboard, drawn up, checked and labelled. Overhead lighting was being positioned and switched on. A suction unit was being tested. Radiographers were donning lead jackets and doctors were tying on disposable gowns and pulling on gloves. Advanced airway care equipment was being assembled and checked.

Belinda Scott, the nurse responsible for the airway equipment, deflated the balloon on the endotracheal tube she had just checked, glancing up to catch Penelope's eye just as the phone was finally answered.

'Jeremy Lane.'

'Hi, Jeremy.' Penelope ignored Belinda's meaningfully raised eyebrow. She also ignored the fact that Chrissy's elbow had just dislodged a box of sixteen-gauge cannulae and sent them scattering over the floor at her feet. She even managed to ignore the familiar tingle the sound of Jeremy's voice engendered. Her tone was entirely professional. 'Penelope Baker speaking, Jeremy. Trauma Room.'

'Penny! My day is improving.' Jeremy's tone was far from professional. Warm. Distinctly inviting. Penelope had to take a somewhat deeper breath.

'We've got a nineteen-year-old multi-system trauma patient coming in. A paragliding accident. Apparently he has neck and head injuries and attempts to intubate in the field were unsuccessful—'

'I'm on my way.' There was no need for Penelope to elaborate. As she summoned his expertise to deal with a potentially life-threatening situation, any hint of flirtation evaporated instantly. Senior anaesthetics registrar Jeremy Lane was now as focused as every member of the emergency resuscitation team. Including Penelope Baker.

'Estimated time of arrival, four minutes,' someone called.

The bustle was subsiding as Penelope turned away from the phone. Chrissy's latest disaster had been rectified and the young nurse now stood out of harm's way in the corner, her cheeks still flushed scarlet. The preparations in the trauma room were now complete. Both the inner swing doors and the outside doors leading to the ambulance loading bay stood open. The trauma team stood, gowned and gloved, awaiting the arrival of their patient.

Penelope breathed in deeply, soaking in the atmosphere of calm control with the undercurrent that only high levels of adrenaline could produce. This was the part of her job she loved the most. There was no room now for any unprofessional personal reflection. She was simply a member of a highly trained medical team waiting for a chance to do what gave them all the highest level of satisfaction.

Waiting to save a life.

The ambulance backed swiftly and smoothly up to the loading bay of Wellington's St Margaret's Hospital. The doors opened immediately and the stretcher was lifted from the vehicle, raised and wheeled directly to the trauma room. The patient was strapped to a backboard which made the transfer to the bed a swift procedure.

'On the count of three. One…two…three.'

Belinda unhooked the oxygen tubing from the portable cylinder and reattached it to the overhead supply outlet. Penelope lifted the bag of intravenous fluid out of the way of the approaching shears as clothing was cut away from the patient. She hung the bag on a hook near the oxygen outlet and opened the flow enough to keep the line patent then stepped to one side to make room for the staff members who were attaching the electrodes needed for a 12-lead electrocardiogram and wrapping an automatic blood-pressure cuff around their patient's upper arm.

The noise level in the trauma room rose as equipment was manoeuvred and the team focused on gathering the observations and information they required immediately.

Penelope moved swiftly back to her position at the drugs trolley. Extra drugs that might be required needed drawing up and labelling. Despite the level of concentration the task entailed, Penelope was still able to assimilate most of what was happening around her.

'The patient's name is Richard Milne. He's nineteen years old.' Information previously relayed by radio needed repetition and clarification by the ambulance staff. 'He got blown off course while para-gliding and landed in a tree.'

'BP's 140 over 80.' Belinda was able to keep an eye on the monitor screens from her position at the head of the bed.

'What gauge IV access do we have?' Emergency Department registrar Mark Wallace was checking the patency of the cannulation done by the para-medics.

'Fourteen.'

'Let's get another line in.'

Penelope watched the circulation nurse collect and deliver the supplies Mark would need. Chrissy was also watching carefully as another bag of IV fluid was set up and the giving set attached and primed with no hint of any tangles in the tubing.

'He tried to get himself out of his harness to climb down, slipped and was caught around the neck by the harness as he fell.' A paramedic was speaking to the consultant leading the medical team, Jack Hennessey. 'He hung long enough to lose con-sciousness, then the branch broke and he fell ap-proximately six metres. The fall was broken to some extent by lower branches and he landed on a grassed area.'

'Was he wearing a helmet?'

The helmet was in the hands of a second ambu-lance officer. 'It's damaged at the back,' he reported. 'Witnesses didn't think he was KO'd.'

'He was conscious on our arrival,' the paramedic continued. 'Glasgow Coma Score 14. No neurological deficit. Fractured mid-shaft femur on the left side and a fractured right wrist. GCS dropped *en route* to 10 with increasing respiratory distress.'

Penelope glanced towards the patient's head. The level of consciousness was still well down. The teenager's eyes remained closed and his verbal responses were limited to an occasional moan. The neck collar had now been removed and Belinda Scott was providing manual stabilisation while Jeremy assessed the injury to the neck and the patency of the patient's airway. Air movement was not good. Penelope could hear the girl's harsh inhalations clearly through the general noise level. She could also hear Jeremy Lane speaking to the consultant.

'We've got some major oedema here. Trachea's still midline and there's no subcutaneous emphysema on the neck but I can't rule out a tracheal rupture.'

'Oxygen saturation is down to 85 per cent.'

Jack Hennessey turned to Mark Wallace. 'See if you can get an arterial blood gas off after you've secured that IV line.' He looked back at Jeremy. 'Are you going to intubate?'

'I'll have a go. Could do with fibreoptic endoscopy, judging by the oedema present, but it won't be the first time I've done it blind.' Jeremy sounded confident. 'Could I have someone ready for cricoid pressure? Thanks.'

Penelope looked at the registrar standing beside her at the drugs trolley. Labelled syringes were spread out in front of them, including sedation and paralysis agents and cardiac drugs in case prolonged laryngoscopy led to a deterioration in heart function. Duplicate ampoules were readily available. The registrar acknowledged their readiness with a nod.

'You do it, Penny. I'm all set.'

Belinda was still holding the patient's head in a position to protect his neck. A cervical spine injury had not yet been ruled out. Jeremy was hyperventilating their patient with rapid squeezes on the bag mask unit. A neuromuscular blocking agent was administered and then Penelope positioned her fingers on the young man's neck to press on the cricoid cartilage. With the amount of soft tissue swelling this wasn't as easy as Penelope would have liked but she was confident she had located the correct spot. She knew that pressure on this part of the Adam's apple reduced the risk of vomiting and aspiration during the procedure. It also displaced the larynx and aided visualisation for Jeremy.

In this instance it wasn't enough of an aid. Jeremy had two attempts to pass the intubation tube into the trachea.

'This is hopeless,' he pronounced. 'Bag him, will you, Penny? The suxamethonium won't wear off for a while yet. We might have to go for a tracheostomy here.'

Penelope fitted the face mask securely and squeezed the bag to provide oxygen to the now paralysed teenager.

'What about a needle cricothyroidotomy?' Jack Hennessey suggested. 'The injury seems to be above the level of the larynx.'

'That would only give us thirty to forty minutes' effective ventilation. This lad's going to need CT scanning to rule out a skull fracture and C-spine injury before he even gets near the operating theatre.'

'Heart rate's dropping. Down to 90,' a nurse warned.

'And pulse pressure's widening. One-fifty over 95.'

Tension in the trauma room went up a notch. The signs could be a warning of rising intracranial pressure from an as yet undiagnosed injury. Airway control and adequate ventilation had to be instigated as quickly as possible.

'Surgical cricothyroidotomy should be enough.' Mark joined the discussion between Jack and Jeremy. 'Fewer complications than a tracheostomy, which could be done later in Theatre if it's needed.'

'Are you happy to do it?'

Mark nodded. He glanced at Jeremy. 'Unless you want to?'

Jeremy shrugged. 'Go for it, mate. I'll look after the bag mask and Penny can assist you.'

Penelope relinquished the ventilation equipment, taking a quick glance at Jeremy as she did so. Was he bothered by his unusual failure to intubate a patient? Less than happy to hand over the imminent procedure to a newcomer? If so, he didn't show it. Jeremy smiled at Penelope.

'Seen one of these done before, Penny?'

'No, but I know where the kit is. I'll find it.'

She opened the roll of sterile drape on top of a fresh trolley to reveal the sterilised equipment that would be needed.

'Clean the whole area over the cricoid and thyroid cartilage,' Mark directed her. 'Then we'll infiltrate with one per cent plain lignocaine.'

Penelope swabbed the young man's neck.

'I'm going to stabilise the thyroid cartilage here,' Mark told the onlookers. 'Then I make a horizontal incision over the cricothyroid membrane. Scalpel, please.'

Everyone in the trauma room was crowding in for a closer look. This wasn't an everyday occurrence. Mark appeared confident as he cut carefully into their patient's throat. He reversed his hold on the scalpel and inserted the handle.

'It's helpful to rotate it through ninety degrees to open the airway,' he explained. 'Can I have a size 9 endotracheal tube, now, please?'

The tube that Penelope handed him was carefully inserted and the cuff inflated. Penelope had the sutures ready to hand over next. She watched as Mark stitched the tube into place.

'I'll get us hooked up.' Jeremy was adjusting controls on the ventilator. 'Let's see if we can get some better-looking oxygen saturation figures.' He nodded at Mark. 'Well done.'

'Thanks.' With the airway and breathing for their patient now under control, Mark's attention was diverted. He was examining Richard's chest for injuries and had his stethoscope in his ears to recheck breathing.

'Let's have another neurological check,' Jack requested. 'What are the pupils like?'

'Equal and reactive. Bit more sluggish than they were.'

'Let's run off a C-spine, chest and pelvic set of films,' Jack directed. 'Then we'll send him for a CT scan of his head and neck.' He was watching Mark as the registrar took a moment to re-examine their patient's abdomen. He glanced at Penelope. 'Give Neurology a call and get someone down for a consult, will you, please? Don't worry about Orthopaedics just yet. That femur and wrist can wait.'

The doctors moved back as the radiographers positioned equipment.

'Chest and abdomen look OK,' Mark informed Jack. 'I'd say he's pretty stable for the moment.'

'Now that we've got that airway sorted out, he is. Nice job, there, Mark.'

'Thanks.' Mark was looking at Penelope. 'Thanks for your help. Penny, isn't it?'

'Penelope Baker.' Penelope wanted to add her compliments about the surgical intervention but, while Mark smiled at her briefly, his attention was obviously still on their patient. He reached for a lead jacket so he could move back while the X-rays were being taken.

'How bad is that femur?'

'Feels like a clean break. Minimal swelling thanks to the traction splint. There's a Colles' fracture of the right wrist but everything else is superficial. With a bit of luck we might even keep him out of Theatre.'

'What's wrong with Theatre?' Jeremy appeared relaxed as he joined the other doctors. He winked at Penelope as Mark moved away. 'I'm quite happy in there myself.' A glance at the wall clock prompted a frown. 'In fact, I should be in there right now.'

Jack nodded. 'Mark can take over monitoring the ventilation. Thanks for your help, Jeremy.'

Penelope watched the senior anaesthetics registrar leave the room. An Australian, Jeremy Lane had only taken up his new position at St Margaret's a couple of months ago but Penelope had noticed him the first time he had come into the emergency department. Tall, blond and lean, Jeremy looked as though he'd spent a lot of his time on Australian beaches to acquire that tan. Maybe a lot of time surfing or swimming as well to gain the muscular build that Penelope hadn't been the only one to notice. Neither had she been the only one to notice the fact that the anaesthetist wore no wedding ring.

Penelope swallowed a small sigh. Jeremy was undeniably good-looking and she didn't mind that he had left the trauma room now without a backward glance. The wink had been sufficient for the moment. Jeremy had also made sure that she'd had front-line involvement in the unusual procedure. Penelope was rapt. This had been an exciting resuscitation and it looked as though their young patient was not only going to survive: he might even come through relatively unscathed.

'We've finished here,' a radiographer called. 'We'll have the films through on screen in a minute.'

'Right. We'll tidy up our secondary survey and get things moving,' Jack directed. 'Let's have a few extra hands here for a log roll.'

'Wasn't that awesome? Imagine just cutting into someone's throat like that.'

'Mmm.' Penelope dropped the bloodied scalpel into the sharps disposal container and put the holder with the other instruments destined for resterilisation. 'You'd better put the mask from the bag mask unit in with this lot, Bindy.'

Belinda Scott pulled the mask free from the unit. 'He's good, isn't he?'

'Who?'

'Mark Wallace. Our new registrar.'

'Mmm.' Penelope turned her attention to the suction unit. She stripped off the disposable tubing, coiling it up as she reached for the biohazard rubbish bag. 'I wonder why Jeremy didn't do the cricothyroidotomy?'

'Maybe he didn't know how,' Belinda suggested wickedly. Penelope's dismissive snort made her grin. 'Come on, that's your cue for telling me how wonderful Dr Lane is...yet again!'

Penelope remained silent. She rolled up soiled drapes and stuffed them into the contaminated linen holder. The two nurses were alone as they cleared up the trauma room. The highly equipped area needed to be made completely ready for any new incoming emergency. If Richard Milne returned to the emergency department after his CT scan he would go into another area, but it was more likely that he would be transferred directly to the intensive care unit.

Belinda watched Penelope for a moment before returning to her task of restocking the drug cupboard. Then she shook her head with an expression of fond exasperation.

'For goodness sake, Pen. If you feel this strongly about the man, then *do* something about it.'

'Like what?'

'Ask him out.'

Penelope's jaw dropped. 'Are you kidding? I couldn't do that!'

'Why not? I would.'

'You would, too.' Penelope eyed her friend enviously. 'Why can't I be more like you?' The frustrated shake of her head made the shoulder-length tumble of black curls bounce.

'You'll just have to try harder.' Belinda raised her eyebrows. 'Remember our New Year's resolution? It was you, after all, who proposed we swear off men for life. "Who needs them?" you said. With great conviction, I seem to remember.'

'I'd had rather a lot to drink,' Penelope reminded her. 'And it was only a month after Greg had gone back to what's-her-name.'

'Sharon,' Belinda supplied helpfully. 'Greg dumped you and took off with his old girlfriend and you were unbearably miserable.'

'I wasn't!'

Belinda smiled at the scowl she was receiving. 'I should know. I was the one who had to live with you.' She turned to lock the drug cupboard. 'He'd ruined your life, you said.'

'I've recovered.'

'Yes. With the help of our New Year's resolution.

You've been doing rather well so far. Don't weaken.'

'It *is* November, Bindy.'

'Almost Christmas,' Belinda agreed. 'And then it'll be New Year again.' She grinned widely. 'We can renew our vows.'

Penelope sighed. 'How do you do it? You act like you don't give a damn, and men can't stay away from you.'

'It's because I'm not acting. I *don't* give a damn and neither should you, Pen. Love 'em and leave 'em—like they do to us. No strings.'

'Maybe I want strings. I'm thirty, Bindy. I'm an aunt five times over. Five and a half times actually, and now it's my baby sister who's expecting a baby.'

'How is Rachael?' Belinda seemed eager to be diverted from the depressing direction of Penelope's thoughts. 'She hasn't been around to the flat for ages.'

'I haven't seen much of her since she got pregnant.' Penelope bit her lip. 'Maybe I'm jealous,' she confessed. 'Rachael's three years younger than me and she has everything I've always wanted. A fantastic husband, a great job, a baby on the way and…and blonde hair.'

Belinda laughed. 'So—bleach your hair!'

'Tried that when I was fifteen.' Penelope snorted. 'It looked totally disgusting.' She shook her head.

'That was half a lifetime ago. Do you know, my mother had four children all going to school by the time she was my age?'

'Fate worse than death,' Belinda stated cheerfully. 'I should know. Been there, done that.'

'You didn't have any kids.'

'No, thank goodness.' Belinda reached to switch off the overhead lights. 'Look, Pen, you can have a baby when you're in your forties these days. You've got another whole decade of freedom.'

'I don't want freedom,' Penelope responded with conviction. 'I want...' She sighed heavily. 'I want Jeremy Lane.'

'Fine.' Belinda sounded decisive. 'You can have him.'

Penelope grinned, pausing as she headed for the doors pushing a linen bag. 'How?'

'Leave it with me. I'll think of something.' Belinda followed Penelope out of the trauma room. 'Just don't marry the man.'

'Why not?'

'Well, are you planning to change your name when you get married?'

'Probably.' Penelope skirted the ambulance stretcher waiting by the sorting desk. A middle-aged man was holding a blood-soaked towel under his nose. 'Why?'

'Have you considered what your name would be if you married Jeremy?'

'Shh!' Penelope's glance around them was anxious but the emergency department staff were all gainfully employed at enough of a distance not to overhear Belinda's indiscreet query. Still, Penelope kept her voice well down, unable to resist a response. 'Penelope Lane,' she whispered. 'What's wrong with that?'

'"*Penny* Lane"? You know—the Beatles' song?' Belinda began humming loudly.

'Go away, Bindy.' Penelope couldn't help laughing. 'I've got work to do.'

Penelope was still smiling as she moved back to the sorting desk. Her name was on the whiteboard to take the next patient and it looked like she had a nosebleed to sort out. She had to concede that Penny Lane might be a name that could cause some amusement but Penelope Lane had a much more dignified ring to it.

In fact, it had a very nice ring to it indeed.

CHAPTER TWO

THERE was something distinctly unsettling about pale-coloured eyes.

These were pale blue eyes with a darker rim that seemed to emphasise the intensity of the stare that Penelope was receiving.

'What's your name?'

'Penny.' Penelope glanced at the booking-in paperwork in her hand. 'And you're Aaron, aren't you?'

He nodded without returning the smile. 'Aaron Jacobs. Do you like being a nurse?'

'Of course. It's my job. Come this way, Aaron. Have you been waiting long?'

'It doesn't matter. I know how busy you guys are. Where are we going?'

'Cubicle 10. It's this way.'

'What's going to happen? Are you coming with me, Penny?'

'I'm going to be your nurse,' Penelope confirmed. 'I'll check you out and then one of the doctors will come to see you. It's your wrist that you've hurt, isn't it?' She glanced at the tall, lanky young man walking beside her. His right hand cradled his left elbow, the injured wrist and hand tucked inside a faded and grubby denim jacket.

'That's right. I whacked it with a hammer.'

'Accidentally, I hope!' Penelope laughed and her patient finally smiled at her. 'Here we are, Aaron. Let's get your jacket off so I can see your wrist and then I'll get you to climb up on the bed.'

Penelope unbuttoned the cuffs of the jacket and eased it carefully off the injured side. The left wrist looked very swollen, a nasty pale lump with an inflamed red edge at the base of the thumb.

'You've certainly given that a good thump,' Penelope observed. 'What were you using? A sledgehammer?'

Aaron smiled again as he climbed up to sit on the edge of the bed. He held his left arm out towards Penelope. 'It hurts,' he informed her.

'I'm not surprised. Can you wiggle your fingers?'

Aaron complied with a groan. 'That hurts, too.'

Penelope took hold of the hand gently. 'Can you squeeze my fingers?'

The pressure was surprisingly firm. 'That's pretty good.' Penelope nodded. 'OK, you can let go now.'

'Do you like being a nurse?'

Penelope's nod was brisk. She took a careful breath, trying to detect any recent alcohol consumption on her patient's part. It wasn't just that Aaron was repeating the question he had asked only minutes before. There was something about his stare that was vaguely disturbing.

'Nurses help people, don't they?'

'They do.' Penelope picked up the clipboard and pen lying on the end of the bed. 'I need to write a few more details for the doctor here, Aaron. How old are you?'

'Twenty-five. How old are you, Penny?'

'A lot older than you.' Penelope wasn't going to encourage a personal conversation. 'What were you doing at the time of your accident?'

'Knocking a hole in my wall.'

'And what happened?'

'I was holding a bit of wood that got stuck. I aimed a really big hit at the end of it but I missed.'

'What time did this happen?'

'Dunno. I don't wear a watch.'

'Was it this afternoon?'

'Yeah. Couple of hours ago, I guess.'

About the time that the resuscitation on Richard Milne had been in full swing. Penelope's thoughts were diverted momentarily as she wondered how the young paraglider was doing. There had been no time to follow up any developments because of the stream of minor cases she'd had under her care. No opportunities to talk to Belinda or even think about the plans her friend might be hatching to get her a little closer to Jeremy. Penelope sighed lightly. No chance of having to call in an anaesthetics registrar for this patient. She pulled the blood-pressure stand towards the bed.

'I'm going to take your blood pressure, Aaron. I need to wrap this cuff around your arm. Can you pull your shirtsleeve up for me, please?'

'Sure.'

Penelope had to stand closer to her patient as she applied the cuff. She avoided eye contact but she could feel his gaze on her.

'You're beautiful, Penny.'

Penelope's smile was extremely brief. She fitted the earpieces of her stethoscope into place and positioned the disc on the inside of Aaron's elbow, apparently concentrating on her task. The vital sign measurement was automatic, however, and Penelope's thoughts strayed again. Did Jeremy think she was beautiful? He had certainly managed to make her feel attractive over the last few weeks but did she have genuine cause to believe that? The comments had been few in reality but treasured all the more for their rarity.

Like the day she hadn't tried to tame her wildly curly black hair into its usual short ponytail. She had just taken a section from the front at both sides and drawn them into a small plait at the back, leaving the rest of her curls to cover her ears with the ends just touching her shoulders. Rules about hairstyles were much more relaxed these days and the only comment she had received had been from Jeremy.

'Love your hair like that,' he'd said. 'It really suits you.'

Penelope had been wearing her hair exactly like that ever since. Had Jeremy noticed? She released the valve on the sphygmomanometer. 'One-twenty over 80,' she informed Aaron. 'Perfectly normal.' Penelope placed her fingers on her patient's wrist, her gaze now fastened on the second hand of her watch. 'I'll just check your pulse now, Aaron.'

He was still staring at her with those oddly pale eyes. Penelope's eyes weren't pale. What was it Jeremy had said? It hadn't been long after she'd met him for the first time. She had been doing the cricoid pressure on an intubation that Jeremy had been called in for. A very obese woman who'd suffered a major stroke. That had been a difficult case to intubate as well and their heads had been very close together at one stage during the procedure. Successfully completed, Penelope had been assisting in tying the endotracheal tube firmly into place and Jeremy had caught her eye. His voice had been low enough not to be overheard by the other staff members nearby.

'Do you realise,' he'd murmured, 'that your eyes are exactly the colour of the delphiniums my mother used to grow in her garden?' Jeremy had smiled at her, holding the eye contact for another split second. His final comment had been almost inaudible. 'My favourite flowers.'

Penelope recorded the baseline heart and respiration rate she had now completed on Aaron Jacobs. She had the feeling her own rates had just increased significantly thanks to the direction of her straying thoughts. She turned her attention firmly back to the task in hand.

'Do you have any other medical conditions you're being treated for, Aaron?'

'Asthma,' he responded. 'I've got a Ventolin inhaler but I don't need it very often.'

'Anything else?'

'No.'

'Are you allergic to any medications?'

'No.'

'How bad is the pain in your wrist at the moment?'

'Pretty bad.'

'On a scale of zero to ten, with zero being no pain and ten being the worst you could imagine, what score would you give it?'

'About an eight.'

'OK. I'll see about getting you something to help with that. You're going to need your wrist X-rayed to make sure you haven't broken anything and then a doctor will come and see you.' Penelope pulled back the cubicle curtain. 'You might have a bit of a wait, I'm afraid. We're quite busy today.'

'That's cool. I don't mind waiting. Will you come back to look after me?'

'I'll be back as soon as I've organised some pain relief for you. There's a buzzer beside the bed if you need it and I won't be too far away. I've got other patients I need to take care of as well.'

Aaron settled back onto his pillow. 'Leave the curtain open, won't you?' he requested. 'That way I'll be able to see you when you go past.'

Penelope complied, although she didn't much like the thought of Aaron Jacobs watching out for her. She would try and make sure she didn't need to go past cubicle 10 too often. Penelope almost smiled wryly at the thought. If it had been Jeremy in cubicle 10 she would have been walking past as often as possible—like she did when he was in the emergency department and she hadn't been lucky enough to be involved in whatever case he had been called in for. She enjoyed providing a distraction almost as much as working with the man. Funny how you knew when someone was watching you even when you were being deliberately casual and not looking in their direction.

Penelope headed for cubicle 2. Perhaps Mrs Jennings was back from her ultrasound now and the provisional diagnosis of fibroids had been confirmed, which would explain the profuse intermenstrual bleeding the middle-aged woman was experiencing. Mrs Jennings was probably going to need admission in any case due to her severe anaemia. Cubicle 2 was still empty but Penelope took a minute to tidy up. Packaging and used IV supplies had been discarded on top of the locker after IV fluid replacement had been initiated. It was easy to let her attention wander again from such an automatic task.

Penelope's thoughts had come full circle now. On balance, she did believe that Jeremy found her attractive. Maybe even beautiful. She hadn't believed it at first. A lot of new doctors were inclined to flirt and it took time to decide whether that was simply the way they treated all the women in their orbit. Jeremy had never made any personal comments to other nurses that Penelope had overheard, however, and Belinda had told her he'd never shown the slightest interest in her. Surely if Jeremy was that way inclined then Penelope's flatmate would have been a prime target. Belinda was gorgeous—tall and slim, with the combination of a long mane of red-gold hair and bright green eyes that were enough to send most male newcomers into a spin.

Yes. Penelope had every reason to believe that, for some obscure reason, Jeremy had singled her out to feel special…and she did. For the first time in longer than Penelope cared to remember she felt special, attractive. Desirable, even… And it felt *so* good. Greg's blatant rejection in favour of what's-her-name had been the last of a long run of romantic disasters. Penelope's self-esteem and any belief in her desirability had hit rock bottom with a resounding clunk. It was no wonder she had fallen in love with Jeremy.

Penelope stopped with a lurch, halfway to the rubbish bin, her hands full of empty packaging. The inside of a used-up roll of tape fell and bounced on the linoleum. Was she actually in love with Jeremy Lane? In love with a man she hadn't even kissed? Penelope thought about that tingle she got every time she heard his voice. The way her skin could feel when he was watching her. That feeling that was a bit more than a tingle—the one that always started low down in her abdomen when their eyes made contact. She could feel it now, just thinking about it, and it was strong enough to be unmistakable. Sheer physical desire. Penelope knew herself well enough to know she didn't feel that way unless she was seriously in love.

The rubbish fitted neatly into the bin and Penelope stooped to retrieve the cardboard ring left over from the roll of adhesive tape. Yes. She was definitely in love with Jeremy and it was time things moved ahead. It shouldn't be difficult if his attraction to her was genuine. Maybe Belinda was right. Or sort of right. There was no way Penelope could take the initiative by asking *him* out. That would be risking a rejection that could possibly be even more painful than Greg's defection. There had to be a way of setting up an opportunity that Jeremy couldn't miss—not just one that he wouldn't want to miss.

Not if he felt the same way she did. Belinda was bound to have some good ideas.

Penelope's quick scan confirmed that cubicle 2 was acceptably tidy. She would see about some medication for Aaron Jacobs and if Mrs Jennings still wasn't back from her ultrasound she'd grab a few minutes for a coffee. With a bit of luck, Belinda might be having a quiet spell and they could talk. That way Penelope wouldn't have to wait until she got home that night to hatch a plan. She didn't want to wait. Buoyed by her analysis of Jeremy's genuine interest, Penelope felt a new confidence blooming. The time was right. The man was right. All that was needed was a way of pulling it all together.

Disappointingly, Belinda was heading away from the staffroom when Penelope arrived ten minutes later.

'I was hoping to catch you. Have you finished your break?'

'Nope. Just starting.' Belinda held up a polystyrene cup full of coffee. 'I've got ten minutes. I'm heading outside for a spot of fresh air. My last patient was a rectal bleed.'

'Yuck.' Penelope grimaced sympathetically. The smell that accompanied such a patient was as distinctive as it was unpleasant. 'I'll get my water out of the fridge and join you. I could do with some fresh air myself.'

The view of an overcrowded car park was not

attractive and the breeze was chilly, but it was always good to escape completely if only briefly during a busy shift. It gave them a chance to forget professional matters for a few minutes. It was also a chance for Penelope to pay attention to her more personal preoccupation.

'I think you're right, Bindy,' she announced.

'Of course I am.' Belinda grinned. 'What about, in particular?'

'Jeremy. It's time to do something.'

Belinda raised an eyebrow. 'You're going to ask him out?'

'No way.' Penelope shook her head decisively. 'He's going to ask *me* out. I just need to set it up.' Her smile was hopeful. 'I'm sure he will. If he wasn't interested he wouldn't say the things he does. And he wouldn't keep giving me those *looks*.'

'Hmm.' Belinda didn't sound convinced. 'He could be toying with you, you know. He might just be playing the game of getting *you* interested to prove to himself that he still has what it takes. He's no spring chicken.'

'He's not exactly old. Thirty-eight maybe. Or forty.'

'Probably forty-five,' Belinda decided. 'Grey hairs are less obvious on blonds.' She sipped her coffee thoughtfully. 'I suppose he's not bad-looking but he's not the only one. That new registrar of ours isn't bad either. What's his name?'

'Mark Wallace.' Penelope shrugged. She hadn't taken much notice of Mark in the few days he'd been in the department. He had certainly performed impressively this morning, however, with the emergency procedure on the young paraglider. Penelope was easily diverted. 'How's Richard doing? Have you heard?'

'He's in Intensive Care. Apparently the CT scan didn't show up any major brain damage or injury to the trachea and the swelling is going down with the ice packs and anti-inflammatory treatment. They're going to set the fractures later today and they'll take him off ventilation as soon as they're sure the swelling is under control. I think he's going to be fine.'

'That's fantastic.' Penelope's smile was very satisfied. 'He could have died. Great case, wasn't it?'

'Yeah.' Belinda drained her coffee-cup, checked her watch and sighed. 'Two more minutes. I'm ready to go home.'

Penelope sighed as well. Belinda hadn't been as supportive as she'd hoped so far. 'What am I going to do, Bindy? About Jeremy, I mean?'

'Let him think you haven't got the slightest interest in him,' Belinda advised. 'Find someone else. There's a new rotation of house-surgeons in there. Some of them are quite tasty.'

'Bindy!' Penelope would have been genuinely shocked if she hadn't known her friend so well. She still shook her head in mild disapproval. 'You can't go round eyeing up every man that comes into the emergency department as a potential plaything.'

'Why not? You can bet your boots that's exactly what they're doing to us.' Belinda crumpled the polystyrene cup. 'Come on. Back to the salt mines.'

'I don't want to just play.' Penelope followed Belinda reluctantly. 'I want something real.'

'And you really think that Jeremy is the real thing?'

Penelope's nod was solemn.

'In that case, you need to spend some time away from work with him. Have a few drinks somewhere. Meet up at a party.'

Penelope nodded again, more happily this time, as the nurses skirted the car park. This sounded like a plan, though not an easily implemented one.

'Nobody's having parties at the moment. The weather's still a bit iffy for barbecues and it's too early for the Christmas rush.'

'We could have a party.'

'In our flat? We'd be lucky to squeeze six people into our living room.'

'Hmm.' Belinda paused as they reached the ambulance bay. 'Where does he live?'

'Nowhere. He asked me to go house-hunting with him a couple of weeks ago, remember?'

'Oh, yes. The day he didn't show up.'

'He got called in.'

'So he said. After he'd left you moping around, waiting all day.'

'He couldn't ring.' Penelope had to defend Jeremy. 'He was in Theatre.'

Belinda's expression was enough to remind Penelope that even operating theatres were equipped with telephones but she didn't press her point. 'He must live somewhere.'

'He's got a room in "The Hovel".'

'Aha! Excellent.'

'Why?' While the nickname for the huge, old house that had been converted to single doctors' quarters dated from the days before extensive renovation, it was still not generally considered the most desirable residence.

'There's a bar downstairs. What time do you finish today?'

'Six o'clock.'

'Even better. I'm off at six-thirty. We'll go and park ourselves in the bar. He's bound to float past and we'll nab him and offer him a drink.'

'We can't just go into the bar. It's for residents only.'

'And their guests. Matt Greenway is living there and he's been after me to have a drink with him for weeks. Consider yourself invited, my friend. Wear something sexy.'

'I don't *do* sexy. I've only got my jeans here, anyway.'

'Jeans can be very sexy.'

'Only on a figure like yours. On mine, jeans are practical.'

'What else did you wear in this morning? I can't remember.'

'Red jumper, white shirt.'

'The red jumper's good. Nice neckline. Ditch the shirt, though. Much sexier with nothing underneath.'

'I'll itch.'

The ambulance backing into the bay was a reminder that the two nurses had extended their break for too long. Belinda gave Penelope an exasperated glance. 'Look, Penny—do you want to do something about him or not?'

'Of course I do.'

'Well, this is it. The best plan I can come up with. The rest is up to you.'

'OK.' Penelope took a very deep breath. 'I'll do it. No shirt.'

The plan had got off to a wonderful start. Matt Greenway seemed delighted to have Penelope's company if it gave him a chance to spend time with Belinda. There were enough other people in the bar to make the atmosphere casual and Jeremy did, indeed, float past. Belinda took her cue perfectly.

'Jeremy! Come and join us. You can give us an update on our paraglider.'

Jeremy nodded at Belinda and smiled warmly at

Penelope. 'I'll get a drink and be right with you,' he promised.

Now, however, the wheels appeared to have fallen off the plan. Jeremy had his drink but he wasn't moving away from the bar. He was deep in conversation with Mark Wallace.

Belinda looked annoyed. She nudged Penelope. 'You'll have to go over there,' she whispered, 'and break it up.'

Penelope was disconcerted. 'How?'

'Go and get us some more drinks. Join the conversation and then steer Jeremy over here. Tell him I'm waiting to hear about our patient.'

Penelope moved before she had time to get nervous. The barman smiled at her.

'Same again?'

Penelope nodded. She was listening to the conversation between the two men beside her.

'I would have gone for a tracheostomy myself. We couldn't be sure that the injury level was entirely above the larynx.'

'It was worth a try. I've been taught to save tracheostomy for a last resort. There's a high morbidity and the associated mortality risk is about three per cent. That's not insignificant. I saw a burns patient die having one attempted a while back, and it left a major impression on me.'

The barman was sliding glasses across the bar towards Penelope. 'Two white wines and one lager. Is that the lot?'

'Yes, thanks.'

Jeremy turned at the sound of Penelope's voice. 'Penny. This is a lovely surprise. What brings you into The Hovel?'

'My friend, Belinda. She was too shy to come by herself.'

Belinda's peal of laughter from the other side of the room sounded anything but shy. Jeremy's smile made Penelope feel as though he had seen through the plan instantly. She tried to ignore the threatened prickle of humiliation by glancing at Jeremy's companion.

'Hi, Mark. Are you living here, too?'

'For the moment. I want to get my own place as soon as I can. I'm going to rent a car tomorrow to have a look at a couple of houses for rent around the harbour. I'd like a sea view.'

'I love the sea, too. I love the smell of salt air and being able to hear the waves at night.' Penelope found herself smiling. Mark was easy to talk to.

'Makes the cars rust,' Jeremy broke in. 'I'd rather be up on the hills and just have the view.'

Penelope turned to collect her change from the barman. Was that how Jeremy saw her, perhaps? As part of a view? Jeremy was making this difficult. If she invited him to join their table now, it could be seen as a very obvious ploy to throw herself at the man. The flash of irritation took Penelope by surprise. So did the memory of a piece of Belinda's advice. Maybe letting Jeremy think she wasn't interested wasn't such a bad idea after all. Maybe letting him think that she might be interested in someone else was an even better idea. Penelope picked up the wineglasses. She smiled at Mark.

'I finish at two tomorrow,' she told him casually. 'If you don't want the hassle of renting a car I'd be happy to play taxi driver. I was born and raised in Wellington so I know my way around.'

'Thanks.' Mark looked delighted. 'I'd really appreciate that, Penny. How 'bout we meet here at two-thirty?'

'I'll be here.' Penelope smiled again and included Jeremy in her glance. 'See you later, Jeremy.'

Belinda's dismayed expression at Penelope returning to their table alone was less pronounced than the one Jeremy had been trying to conceal when she'd left the bar. Penelope smiled reassuringly at Belinda. She'd fill her in later and thank her for having given her the idea in the first place. Plan B had definite possibilities. Penelope stole a glance at the bar and caught Jeremy's thoughtful stare in her direction. She looked away hurriedly and bit back a satisfied smile.

Plan B appeared to be working perfectly already.

CHAPTER THREE

PENELOPE knew she ought to be feeling guilty.

Here she was, heading out on a date with a man who had no idea of the part he was playing in Plan B. But Penelope wasn't feeling guilty at all. In fact, Mark's company was so relaxing she could forget about Plan B and the frustration in her life that had led to its creation. Even the weather was doing its bit to add to a pleasant afternoon. The dark clouds and squalls of heavy spring rain had cleared to leave only cotton-wool puffs scudding across a brilliant blue sky. The stiff breeze was still chilly and Penelope was glad she had chosen to wear her red jumper again—this time with the warmth of a shirt underneath. Woolly socks and trainers on her feet might not be as sexy as the summer sandals she had considered briefly but, then, this wasn't a real 'date'. Merely an outing. A helpful gesture towards a new colleague who was turning out to be very pleasant company.

Mark was driving Penelope's small hatchback car. It had been his own suggestion and Penelope had been happy to hand over the keys. Now she could really relax and enjoy whatever the afternoon had to offer. She loved the drive around the harbour and one of the houses Mark had lined up to view was quite remote—right out past Scorching Bay.

'You need to get into the right-hand lane here,' she directed. 'We want to go through the Mount Victoria tunnel and then follow the main road down to the harbour.' Penelope watched as Mark checked the rear-view mirrors and indicated their lane change.

'It would be at least a twenty-minute drive to the hospital from Scorching Bay,' she warned Mark. 'Probably a lot more in heavy traffic. Won't that be a hassle?'

'Could be worth it,' Mark responded. 'It's not as if we're on call and have to come in to work at a moment's notice. We have set shift hours. Sometimes you need to be able to put real distance between home and work. Especially in a department like ours.'

Penelope agreed readily. Emergency medicine was usually full on. Huge numbers of patients could often take a heavy toll on both professional and personal resources.

'What do you do, Penny? To switch off from work?'

'Sleep mostly.' Penelope laughed. 'And spend time with friends.'

'Any particular friends?' Mark's query was casual but Penelope sensed he was sounding out whether she had a man in her life. She suppressed the pang of guilt firmly.

'Only Bindy. Belinda Scott,' she elaborated in response to the questioning expression Mark gave her. 'She's a nurse in Emergency, too. Tall. Long, reddish hair.'

'Oh, yes.' Mark nodded. He had noticed Belinda. Of course he had. Any man would have noticed Belinda.

'She's my flatmate.'

'Where do you live?'

'We share a townhouse tucked up on Mount Victoria. Right on the border of the park. One of the walkways goes past our back door. Bindy often drags me out running. She's an exercise freak.'

'And you're not?'

'Not really,' Penelope confessed. She looked down at her sturdy, denim-clad legs and her laugh was self-deprecating. 'Can't you tell?'

'No,' Mark responded promptly. He flashed her a sideways grin. 'I'm a bit of couch potato myself. You look just fine to me. Are we still in the right lane here?'

'Yes. There's a big roundabout coming up. We go left and that'll take us onto Shelly Bay Road. Just keep the harbour on your left after that and we can't go wrong.' Penelope stole a glance at her companion. There wasn't much wrong with the way Mark looked even if he was a couch potato, which

was doubtful. He wasn't particularly tall—maybe
five nine or ten—and his shoulders were broad for
his height so he couldn't be considered lean, yet the
impression he gave was one of nice proportions.
Maybe it was his colouring that was appealing. The
black hair and very dark green eyes. Or maybe it
was his laid-back manner. Quiet but confident.
Friendly but thoughtful at the same time. Penelope
had the feeling that Mark's loyalty might not be
given easily but once it was given it would be there
to stay. She liked that. Mark had the makings of
being a good friend.

The silence between them was quite comfortable
but Penelope wanted to talk. She wanted to learn
more about him.

'I've got a sister in Wellington as well. Rachael.
She's the only one in my family left here so I try
and see her as much as I can.' Penelope made a
mental note to call her sister when she got home.
She hadn't tried very hard lately to spend time with
Rachael but it hadn't been until her conversation
with Belinda yesterday that she had realised why she
had been unconsciously avoiding contact. Jealousy
was a poisonous emotion and Penelope had no intention of letting its tentacles gain any more of a
hold on her life. 'Rachael's a vet,' she told Mark
brightly. 'She's three years younger than me and
she's expecting her first baby next year. She and
Tom are very excited.'

'I can imagine.' Mark's smile looked almost wistful. Penelope wondered if he had yearnings for a family himself. Or did he already have one? An ex-wife and a few children tucked away somewhere? He hadn't needed reminding of the direction to take at the roundabout. They headed out along Shelly Bay Road.

'That will make you an aunt,' Mark observed. 'Is that a first for you?'

'Hardly!' Penelope laughed. 'My oldest sister, Sandra, has two children and my brother, John, has three. Sandra lives in Auckland, though, and John's been in Australia for ten years so I've never seen much of those nieces and nephews. Rachael's baby will be the first one I'll have a lot to do with.' It would also be the first pregnancy to watch developing. The first pregnancy to be expected to discuss in intimate detail and the first nursery to help plan. Of course Rachael didn't want to talk about anything else these days. Penelope would have been exactly the same.

'You're very lucky to have such a big family,' Mark told her. 'I was an only child.'

'I wanted to be an only child.' Penelope grinned.

'Why?' Mark sounded astonished.

'Both my sisters are very clever and beautiful. And they've both got blonde hair.' Penelope was still smiling. 'I was the black sheep of the family.'

Mark's glance was admonishing. 'Stop putting

yourself down,' he directed firmly. 'You're an extremely attractive woman.'

'Thanks.' Penelope glanced away in embarrassment. Heavens, she hoped that Mark didn't think she
had been fishing for a compliment. She bit her bottom lip, torn between embarrassment and pleasure.
That was twice in two days that someone had commented positively on her looks. Even if one of them
had been a rather weird patient, it was still flattering.
Penelope let her gaze sweep the harbour with its
usual level of interesting shipping activity as she
tried to think of something casual to say.

The inter-island ferry was just leaving the wharf
on the far side. A huge container ship was waiting
its turn to dock, two tugboats guarding its bows.
Several small fishing vessels were out and a keen
yachtsman in a small craft was making the most of
the stiff breeze, bouncing over the choppy water
close to the road.

'Not the best day for sailing.' Penelope needed to
break the short silence that was vaguely uncomfortable for the first time. She didn't want Mark to think
that he had stepped over a boundary and said something unwelcome. The comment sounded deliberately casual, however, and made Penelope feel more,
rather than less, uncomfortable.

Mark's glance was reassuring. Penelope suspected
he had noticed her discomfort and was quite happy

to take their conversation in whatever direction she preferred.

'It does look a bit rough out there.' Mark's gaze was now back on the road. He was negotiating its frequent turns competently. 'I can see why they've got that metal barrier fence between us and the harbour. This wouldn't be a pleasant drive in really bad weather.'

'No, and Wellington is renowned for delivering plenty of that.'

'So the myth is based on reality? I grew up in the South Island,' Mark told her. 'In Dunedin. We all knew Wellington's reputation for foul weather but I thought it might be exaggerated. Dunedin's not exactly tropical.'

'I'm ashamed to say I've never been that far south,' Penelope confessed. 'We used to have summer camping holidays around Nelson but that's right up the top of the South Island and the weather was always perfect as I remember it.'

'Childhood summer holidays always seem to have had great weather, don't they?' Mark looked thoughtful. 'Maybe we just don't remember the bad stuff. I used to go and stay with some cousins in Central Otago. It was wonderful.'

'Did you do your training in Dunedin?'

Mark nodded. 'I moved to Australia as a registrar and then went to England for a few years. Too long,' he added quietly.

'You didn't like it?'

'The job was great. That's where I fell in love with emergency medicine. Things didn't work out in the end, though.' Mark paused for a second as though considering how much he wanted to say on the topic. An imperceptible shake of his head and a brighter tone to his voice suggested he had chosen a new direction. 'No hope of getting a consultancy there. I would have been a grandfather by the time I stopped being a senior registrar.'

Penelope blinked. 'So you've got children, then?'

'What?' Mark was startled. 'What makes you think that?'

'One generally needs to have kids to become a grandfather. Hard to skip that bit.'

Mark laughed. 'It was just an expression. I've never been married and I haven't got any children, though I certainly hope to one of these days. Hopefully not too far in the future. I'm not getting any younger.'

'Join the club,' Penelope said with feeling. 'I turned thirty earlier this year. It's kind of a major milestone.'

'Hardly remember it,' Mark said cheerfully. 'Wait until you're pushing forty and you'll really have something to worry about.'

'You're not pushing forty, are you?' Penelope's glance was surprised. No hints of significant grey were obvious in Mark's dark hair and the lines around his eyes looked far more attributable to laughter than advancing age.

'I'm thirty-six,' Mark told her. 'Definitely on the downward slide.'

'Yeah, right!' Penelope returned his smile. So. Mark was looking to settle down. He wanted a family. He'd never been married. And here he was starting a new job in a new city and he was living in single quarters. Was he looking for a house because someone significant in his life was planning to join him in Wellington? Somehow, Penelope didn't think this was the case.

'What brought you back to New Zealand?' Penelope found herself asking. 'Besides the lack of career advancement in England.'

'I left England nearly two years ago,' Mark responded after a tiny pause. 'I've been in Auckland but I knew it wasn't where I wanted to settle down. It was just the first job that came up when I decided to leave.' Mark's tone suggested that he'd taken the first escape route that had presented itself. What had he been escaping from? Professional dissatisfaction or something rather more personal? Penelope instinctively knew that it wasn't a subject either of them were ready to discuss. It was time to move back to safer territory.

'You'll find Wellington's weather a bit of a shock after Auckland,' she commented. She cringed slightly as she finished her sentence. Couldn't she think of something more original than the weather for a change of subject?

Mark didn't seem to mind. 'It rains all the time in Auckland,' he said obligingly. 'Very depressing. It's hot and wet.'

'It's cold and wet here.' Penelope smiled. 'And Auckland's storms have nothing on ours. Wellington's storms are unique. Gale-force winds blowing in from Cook Straight and rain that goes sideways.'

'But on a nice day it's perfect,' Mark pointed out. 'It must be one of the prettiest cities in the country with the hills and this harbour.'

'Sure,' Penelope agreed. 'On a nice day it's perfect. All three of them a year,' she added mischievously.

Mark laughed. 'Just as well I enjoy the benefits of bad weather, then.'

'Such as?'

'Roaring log fires. Hot soup. The security of being shut away in a house with the sound of rain beating down on a tin roof.'

The notion of being shut away in front of a roaring fire with Mark wasn't unpleasant. Penelope could almost hear the rain on the roof. She stared ahead in silence for a minute as she allowed herself to enjoy the contemplation. The road opened to a reasonably straight stretch with the next bend well ahead. The barrier fence flashed past on their left, cutting them off from the drop to a narrow, rocky foreshore and steep slope into the water. The breeze was whipping up tiny whitecaps on the surface of the harbour. To their right, the land sloped upwards. The houses were becoming much sparser and many of the dwellings were concealed above gardens of hardy native trees.

Penelope was aware of the child in her peripheral line of vision even as her attention was caught by the large, brightly coloured ball bouncing onto the road well ahead of them.

'Oh, my God!' The words were torn from Penelope as she stared in horror at the rapidly unfolding scene.

The small child followed the ball onto the road just as an oncoming car was rounding the next bend. The driver in the small red hatchback that was a close match to Penelope's own car had no time to brake. Penelope registered the panicked expression on the woman's face as she wrenched at her steering-wheel. Without even slackening its pace, the hatchback swerved onto the other side of the road, heading straight towards Penelope's car. She could feel her seat belt digging in across her body painfully as Mark slammed on the brakes.

Only inches separated Penelope and Mark from the doomed vehicle as it careered past them. The red hatchback was skidding now, any attempt at braking clearly ineffective. Its speed was unabated as it broke through the metal barrier fence marking the harbour side of the roadway. The car was airborne for what seemed like several seconds. Then it hit a large rock before ploughing into the murky grey water of the harbour.

The sound of the impact was shocking, coming in the split second after Mark had brought Penelope's car to a complete halt and the engine had stalled. They were close to the child themselves now. The small girl stood in the middle of the road, bewildered by what was happening. She stuck her thumb in her mouth and gazed unblinkingly at Penelope. Shouting could be heard from the property the child had emerged from. Frantic shouting that indicated the child's mother had seen the accident.

Penelope felt her chin being gripped firmly. She turned her head under the pressure from the fingers holding her to find Mark staring at her intently, his brow furrowed with concern.

'Are you all right?'

'I'm fine.' Penelope's voice came out as a croak. She cleared her throat. 'My God, Mark... The woman in that car...'

'I know.' Mark was unclipping his safety belt. 'Get the child off the road, Penny, and tell her mother to call the emergency services. I'm going to see what I can do.' He paused as he climbed out, reaching to push the hazard light switch. 'Park a bit further down the road and leave the hazard lights on. Flag down anyone that comes past. We might need some more help.'

The reassurance from Mark's instant concern for her own well-being above any others' was enough to galvanise Penelope out of her stunned immobility. She scrambled from the car and scooped up the small girl who was still standing in the middle of the road. A woman was running towards them.

'Tiffany!' The mother's shout ended in a distraught sob. Her arms were outstretched for her daughter as she reached Penelope. 'Is she all right?'

'She's fine. The car didn't touch her.' Penelope handed the child to her mother. The little girl took one look at her mother's face and burst into tears.

'Can you go and ring the emergency services?' Penelope was already turning away. 'I need to shift my car.'

Another vehicle pulled to a halt as Penelope positioned her car. An elderly man rolled down his window. 'What's happened?'

'An accident.' Penelope could see Mark. He had scrambled over the rocks and was now almost waist deep in water. He seemed to be using all his strength to try and open one of the doors of the red car. The attempt was unsuccessful and he began wading rapidly to the other side of the small hatchback.

'I've got a cellphone,' the man told Penelope. 'Shall I ring triple one?'

'Yes.' Penelope didn't know whether the child's

mother would have reached her telephone yet and it wouldn't matter anyway. Better for the emergency services control room to have too many calls than not enough. 'Tell them that the occupant of the car appears to be trapped.'

Penelope climbed over the remains of the metal barrier fence and jumped down onto the rocks below. Thank goodness she had worn her trainers and not sandals. The sturdy footwear provided reasonable grip on the rocks despite the seaweed and algae patches. The water closed around her ankles in an icy grip but Penelope barely registered the discomfort. She pushed through the water with determination. Mark was looking grim, and no wonder. The red hatchback was more than half-full of water and the driver was conscious and screaming.

'Help! *Help!* I can't move. We're going to *drown!*'

We? Penelope could only see one occupant. She reached the car as she listened to Mark's reassuringly firm voice.

'You're not going to drown, Kerry. I'm not going to let that happen, OK? I'm going to have this door open in just a second. Hang on.'

The woman was twisting frantically in the driver's seat. 'I can't see Tommy. Where is he? Oh...*God!*' Another heart-wrenching scream made Penelope flinch.

'What can I do, Mark?'

'Come and help me with this door. It's almost opening. I think it's caught on a rock. I'll go underwater and see if I can shift it. You pull from the top.' Dark green eyes locked onto hers for a brief moment and Mark lowered his voice. 'There's a baby in the back. The car seat's been underwater for nearly a minute.'

Penelope's fingers were already threaded into the gap at the top of the passenger door. 'Quick, Mark,' she urged. 'Let's get this door open.'

Mark took a deep breath, his hand following the line of the door as his head disappeared beneath the surface of the water. A small wave broke against Penelope's back and she braced her feet on the rocks beneath. She could feel movement in the door as Mark tugged from the bottom. Penelope pulled as hard as she could. The door gave another inch or two and then stuck fast. Penelope felt as though she were trying to pull on a concrete wall.

Mark's head broke the surface of the water and he gasped for breath. 'One more go should do it. You're doing great, Penny.' He drew in another ragged breath and disappeared again.

Penelope waited until she felt his renewed efforts. Then she shut her eyes, gritted her teeth and pulled harder than she had ever pulled anything in her life. The door grated and caught, jolted painfully in her hands and then scraped again. Surely now it was open enough to climb inside the car. Penelope sucked in air as she opened her eyes. Her arms were shaking and it was difficult to uncurl her fingers from the car door.

Where was Mark? It had to be well past the time for him to need another breath. Penelope felt cold tendrils of panic clutch at her. Her fear escalated as another wave broke just as the woman in the driver's seat screamed again.

'I can't feel my legs. I'm going to be—' The wave washed through the car, breaking over the woman's face. She gagged and coughed.

Where was Mark? Penelope couldn't see past the solid base of the car door. She could feel the whole car moving jerkily but had no idea what was going on. Had Mark tried to get inside and somehow become trapped himself? Another wave broke against her back and Penelope shouted to make sure the trapped woman could hear her.

'Hold your breath,' she ordered. 'There's another wave coming.'

The splash from the wave was augmented by turbulence as Mark finally surfaced. He shoved something towards Penelope and then turned, clutching at the car door for support as he struggled for breath.

Penelope was holding a baby. A tiny, cold, pale and limp baby. She cradled the infant on her left arm, using her right hand to position the baby's head and open its airway. Then she bent her head, covering the tiny mouth and nose with her own mouth as she blew a careful breath into the small body. She repeated the action, then snapped open the buttons on the front of the soaked stretchsuit the baby was wearing. She tried to feel for a brachial pulse on the tiny upper arm.

Was it her imagination or was there a faint pulse? Penelope bit her lip as she concentrated. Yes! The pulse was there but the baby still wasn't breathing. She gave it another two breaths.

People were beginning to gather on the roadside now and a man was wading towards them. Penelope looked at Mark with concern. He looked very pale and his breathing still sounded ragged.

'The ambulance and fire service are on their way,' the man shouted as he neared them. 'They won't be much longer.'

'The tide's coming in,' Mark warned Penelope. 'We haven't got time to wait. I'm going to try and get Kerry's legs free.'

Penelope couldn't respond with anything more than a nod. She bent over the baby on her arm again, feeling the warmth of her own breath as it entered the tiny mouth. Part of her registered with amazement that Mark could remember and use the name of the trapped woman. Another part was astonished at his courage. Already painfully short of breath himself, he had gone under the surface of that cold, grey water again to try and save the baby's mother. Every wave that came in now was breaking over the woman's face. Sometimes she managed to hold her breath but her panic was making it increasingly difficult.

The stranger had reached Penelope. 'How's the baby?'

Penelope tried the pulse again. It was stronger and faster. The baby jerked as she pressed his arm. Then his face twitched, his mouth opened and his chest heaved convulsively in an attempt to breathe. Penelope tipped the baby over to let any fluid drain from its airways. Then she heard the faint cry like the mewing of a newborn kitten. Astonishingly, the mother had also heard the almost inaudible sound.

'Tommy! Tommy! Oh, God, get me out...*please*! I want my baby.'

'He's OK, Kerry.' The baby's cries strengthened as Penelope turned his face up again. The wailing of a miserable baby had never sounded so welcome.

Mark's head surfaced beside her. He looked grey with exhaustion but something close to a smile appeared as he heard the baby's cries.

'Well done, Pen.' He saw the man beside her. 'See if someone's got a crowbar. I've only got one leg free. Kerry's left foot is wedged under the brake.'

Penelope could see an ambulance approaching the scene at speed with red and blue beacons flashing. She handed the baby to the man.

'Take Tommy,' she directed. 'Give him to the

ambulance officers. Tell them he wasn't breathing when we got him out but he still had a pulse. He's very, very cold.'

'Right.' The man tucked the baby into the folds of the heavy pullover he was wearing. 'I'll see about a crowbar as well.'

The choking sounds from Tommy's mother as a new wave washed through the red car made Penelope catch Mark's gaze with alarm. 'She's going to drown, Mark. We haven't got time to wait for a crowbar.'

'No. We're going to have to try and pull her free. Even if she loses part of her foot it's preferable to drowning.' Mark began taking deep breaths to hyperventilate his lungs.

'I'll come in, too,' Penelope told him. 'I can pull from the back seat.'

Mark shook his head. 'It's too dangerous. There's not much room left for breathing and it would take too long to get out from the back.' He drew in another deep breath and dropped below the surface again.

Penelope stepped over his legs as she ducked and then pulled herself into the back of the car. The wave that broke in her face was terrifying but she concentrated on the woman in the front seat. Kerry had had this terror for far too long now.

'We're going to get you out, Kerry,' she promised. 'Mark's going to pull on your foot. It might hurt but try and help if you can. I'm going to help as well.'

Kerry's head moved but her mouth was under the water now. Her level of consciousness appeared to be dropping and Penelope wasn't sure if Kerry had heard her at all. She had to put her own head underwater in order to get a grip on the woman's left leg. Penelope pulled desperately, trying to co-ordinate her efforts with those she could feel coming from Mark. The thought of the damage to Kerry's foot and the pain they must be causing her had to be suppressed. Kerry now appeared to be unconscious. Even a short time more trapped under the water could be enough to kill her or cause irreversible brain damage.

Penelope's own lungs were burning from the lack of oxygen. She had to surface to breathe. Her strength was fading rapidly. One more tug was probably more than she could manage but she had to have one last try. It took a moment to register that the trapped foot had come free. Penelope felt herself being pushed to the surface. Her head was touching the roof of the car as she dragged in her first breath. And then another. Mark's hand was under her arm, providing firm support. His other arm was holding Kerry's face above the surface of the water. Was she breathing? Penelope couldn't tell. Suddenly, she was cold and exhausted and confused. There was noise all around them. People in uniforms. Loud voices. Hands pulling at the car doors. Hands pulling at her.

The next minutes passed in a haze. Penelope's awareness temporarily focused inwards. She was *so* cold. And *so* tired. Had she waded back to shore herself or had someone carried her? The blankets around her shoulders felt wonderful but why was she sitting in the back of an ambulance? Where was Mark? Penelope blinked, now aware of a sharp anxiety. Was Mark all right? The last thing she could clearly remember was him holding her up inside the car. Holding her and Kerry to make sure they could breathe in the small air pocket still available. He must have been just as cold and exhausted as she had been. More so, even. He had spent far longer under the water than she had. Penelope's head turned first one way, then the other. An ambulance officer looked in the open back door of the vehicle.

'How are you doing, Penny?'

'I'm OK.' It was difficult to speak because of her uncontrollable shivering. 'Where's Mark?'

'I'm here.' Shrouded by blankets, Mark stepped into view. He climbed the back steps of the ambulance and the doors swung shut behind him. 'Kerry's OK. So's Tommy. They're on their way to Emergency.' Mark sat down on the stretcher beside Penelope. 'Now it's your turn. Let me see that arm again.'

'What arm? I'm fine.' Penelope shook her head. 'What are you talking about?'

'You were bleeding quite badly when we got you out of the car.' Mark took Penelope's hand and drew her right arm free of the blankets. To her astonishment, the sleeve of the red jumper was shredded. The jagged laceration to her forearm seemed unreal.

'I don't remember doing that. I didn't feel a thing.'

'I'm not surprised.' Mark's smile was lopsided. 'I doubt whether you were thinking about yourself much at all back there.' He squeezed her hand. 'You were terrific, Pen. I should tell you off for getting into that car but I don't think Kerry would have survived if you hadn't.'

Penelope smiled shakily. She wanted to tell Mark that he had been a lot more terrific than she had been. She had only been following his example. She wanted to tell him that she had never seen anyone doing something as selfless and courageous as that rescue, but the words wouldn't come. Penelope felt far too close to tears and she was still shivering hard enough to make speech difficult. She blinked hard, trying to clear the moisture that was making her vision wobbly, and she could see Mark's smile again. A gentle smile. As gentle as the hug he now pulled her into. His arms felt solid and the warmth of his body was as welcome as the reassurance. Penelope only stirred as she felt the vehicle they were sitting in begin to move.

'Where are we going?'

'Hospital. We both need a hot shower and you need a few stitches in that arm.' Mark stood up, bracing himself against the stretcher. The ambulance officer turned as he noticed Mark's movement.

'Everything OK back there?'

'Where do you keep your dressings? I'll patch up Penny's arm.'

'Overhead locker. You'll find some saline pouches and crêpe bandages up there as well.'

'Wait.' Penelope twisted to look out of the window. She could see fire engines and police cars blocking the roadway. Flashing blue and red lights were everywhere. People were milling about in large numbers and in the middle of it all was her own car. 'What about my car? I can't just leave it here.'

'The police will take care of it.' Mark was pulling supplies from the locker. 'They'll bring it to the hospital. The road is going to be blocked for ages while they get Kerry's car out of the harbour.' He sat down beside her again. 'You're in no fit state to drive anywhere, my love. Just listen to your teeth chattering.' Mark unfolded another blanket and draped it around Penelope's shoulders. 'Now, let me see that arm.'

Penelope stared at Mark but he was concentrating on opening the small pouch of saline to moisten the gauze dressing. Maybe he used endearments when he was talking to all his patients. In which case, she would have to remember to do it herself. It made her feel cared for. As though it was important that she should be taken care of. Obediently, she stuck out her arm.

'Are *you* all right?' Penelope queried. 'Were you hurt?'

'A few bumps and bruises. Nothing a good sleep won't cure.' Mark looked up and caught her gaze. 'To tell you the truth, I feel absolutely shattered.'

'Me, too.' Penelope smiled at Mark. 'But it was worth it, wasn't it?'

'Absolutely.' Mark covered the cut on Penelope's arm with the dressing and began to wind a crêpe bandage into place. 'What does it feel like to be a heroine?'

Penelope's smile widened. 'Probably the same as it feels to be a hero.'

'Some date this turned out to be for you,' Mark said wryly.

Date? Had Mark considered their outing to be a date? Penelope watched the bandage being fastened. Of course it was. She had set it up to look like exactly that for Jeremy's benefit. The thought of Jeremy was intrusive. He didn't belong here and the intrusion was dismissed with remarkable ease.

'It's certainly a date I won't forget in a hurry,' Penelope heard herself admit shyly.

'Let's try and make the next one a little less exciting,' Mark suggested. 'Otherwise we might not survive.'

'OK.' Penelope snuggled further into her blankets. The heating in the ambulance must be on full. The warmth was wonderful even if it wasn't yet enough to stop her shivering. There was something else competing for a spot of being even more wonderful.

Maybe it was the thought of another date with Mark.

CHAPTER FOUR

THE applause was totally unexpected.

Confused, Penelope stopped as she walked through the automatic doors into the emergency department of St Margaret's Hospital. In her state of extreme physical and emotional exhaustion it took several seconds to realise that this loud expression of admiration and appreciation was intended for her. For her and Mark. The whole department had stopped in its tracks as the pair had entered. Consultants, registrars, nurses, students, orderlies and technicians had all paused in their tasks. Even the patients had joined in the spontaneous outburst, probably without knowing why this very wet and tired-looking couple deserved such praise.

The realisation that they had prompted the outburst of applause was overwhelming. Penelope felt tears gather and roll down her face. She shrank back, pulling the now damp blankets tighter around herself, grateful for the firm support of Mark's arm around her shoulders. The wave of applause faded, to be replaced by voices and a press of people delivering hugs, handshakes and congratulations.

'We've heard all about it!'

'Are you both all right?'

'That water must have been *freezing*!'

'We've got hot showers waiting for you.'

'Well done, Penny. You're a heroine.'

'Mark! Couldn't you think of an easier way to impress us quickly?'

'Penny! You've hurt your arm! How bad is it?'

Mark's voice cut through the hubbub. 'It's bad enough to need a bit of suturing but we need to warm up first.'

'She'll need to keep that arm dry.' Consultant Jack Hennessey sounded concerned.

'We can put a plastic bag over it.' Belinda was beside Penelope now, an arm protectively encircling her friend's waist. 'I'll look after her.'

'How's Kerry?' Penelope asked anxiously. 'And the baby?'

'They're going to be fine,' Jack told her. 'Kerry inhaled a bit of sea water so we'll have to watch for aspiration pneumonia. She was hypothermic so we're warming her up now, and the orthopaedic guys are having a look at her foot. There are a few bones broken and she may lose a toe but there's no damage that will affect function.' He smiled at Penelope. 'She's very grateful to be alive. She wants to thank you two.'

Penelope caught Mark's gaze. Neither smiled. They both recognised just how serious the situation had been. If it hadn't been for their efforts Kerry might very well not be alive right now. Only they could know how desperate things had really been. And they had pulled off the rescue. Together.

'And Tommy?' Mark had to clear his throat. 'Is the baby OK?'

'Seems fine.' Jack nodded. 'He's already been checked by Paediatrics. He's alert and pretty hungry, judging by the way he was sounding a few minutes ago.'

'But he was totally unresponsive,' Penelope said. 'He wasn't even breathing spontaneously for ages.'

'Kids can survive some amazing things.' Jack was frowning at Penelope. 'You're as pale as a ghost and you're still shivering. Go and get into that shower, lass.'

'Yes, come on,' Belinda urged. 'You, too, Mark. There's two showers. We've got some scrub suits in the warming cupboard for you both to change into afterwards.'

The hot water was pure heaven. Penelope could feel the chill being drawn from her bones. Her skin turned bright pink and she finally stopped shivering.

'Are you all right in there?' Belinda was waiting outside the door. 'You've been nearly twenty minutes. You'll be turning into a prune.'

'I'm fine,' Penelope responded. 'I'll just rinse the sea water out of my hair.'

'Keep that arm dry,' Belinda reminded her. 'Is it hurting?'

'A bit.' Penelope tilted her head, letting the hot water stream through her curls. 'I'm not looking forward to those stitches.'

'There's a competition going to see who gets to do it.' Belinda sounded delighted. 'Jack and Matt and Mark are still battling it out.' She chuckled. 'There's a resuscitation room waiting for you and it's set up like Theatre. Maybe Jeremy will offer you an anaesthetic.'

'Is Jeremy here?' Penelope turned off the shower hurriedly and reached for a towel. 'Was he called down to see Kerry?'

'No. Apparently he heard about you. The whole hospital is talking about the rescue. There's a newspaper photographer hanging around Reception as well.'

'Oh, help.' Penelope raked at her hair with the fingers of one hand. The mirror in the change room told her how ineffective her effort was likely to be. She looked a mess. Her face was still pale. There were dark circles under her eyes and over-bright pink spots on her cheeks, like a clown's make-up. Her hair was twice as curly as she liked it and she had no comb, let alone any mousse to try and tame it with.

The scrub suit was less than flattering as well. Faded cotton in a shade of green that looked like long-dead moss. Baggy trousers and a shapeless V-necked top that was way too large.

'Sorry.' Belinda grinned. 'There were no small sizes left.'

'That's OK.' Penelope shrugged. 'Right now I couldn't care less how I look. At least I'm warm again.'

Penelope followed Belinda back into the department. Her statement had been quite sincere. She was scrubbed clean of any make-up and her hair was a fright. She wasn't even wearing a bra. Any moment now Jeremy would catch sight of her and Penelope couldn't have cared less how she looked. In fact, she wasn't even remotely excited by the fact that the anaesthetic registrar was in the department. Or by the fact that he had apparently come only to see her. Maybe she was just still too exhausted. The hot shower and return to a normal body temperature had given her a false sense of renewed physical energy. Perhaps her emotional reserves weren't so easily replenished.

'You get to choose, Penny.' Jack was waiting in Resus 2. 'We're all ready to put your arm back together and leave you as unscarred as possible.' He glanced at the registrars flanking him, Matt on his left, Mark on his right. 'Then again, we could always call in someone from Plastics.'

'No.' Penelope shook her head. 'I'm not bothered about a scar on my arm.'

'Thank heaven it wasn't your face.' Jeremy was standing at the head of the bed. His gaze rested on Penelope sympathetically. 'You look...tired, Penny.'

'I am.' Penelope was aware of the vague surprise in Jeremy's expression. Had anyone else noticed the way his gaze had flicked over her whole body before returning to her face and hair? Penelope was tempted to tell him that this was the way she looked first thing every morning.

'Congratulations.' Jeremy's voice cut into her thoughts. 'I couldn't believe it when I heard you single-handedly resuscitated a baby and then dragged its mother from a watery tomb.'

'I didn't,' Penelope said firmly. 'I was just helping the real hero.' She smiled for the first time since entering the resus area, and her smile was directed at Mark.

'Well, I heard differently,' Jeremy insisted. 'And I was really impressed.'

'So was I,' Mark said quietly. 'We can all be very proud of Pen.'

Penelope dropped her gaze. A sneaking delight crowded out her embarrassment. Was Mark proud of her efforts? She was proud of them herself but, then, she had been inspired. Any heroic efforts on her part had been because she hadn't wanted to let Mark down in his determination to save Kerry and her baby. He had earned her loyalty by his own actions and attitude and he would have it again if he ever asked. She wanted to impress this man. Wanted him to feel proud of her.

Penelope turned towards the bed, avoiding any eye contact with Jeremy. She wouldn't have minded particularly if this scar-to-be had been on her face. For once, she felt worthwhile for something far more genuine than what she looked like. And it felt *so* good. Penelope climbed up to sit on the bed and held out her bandaged forearm.

'I'm ready,' she announced. 'Do your worst.'

'So, who's it going to be?'

'I should do it,' Mark said decisively. 'I feel responsible, after all. If I had been a bit more forceful I could have stopped her climbing inside that wreck.'

'Really?' Jeremy sounded cool.

'If I hadn't got in, it might have been too late,' Penelope said quietly. 'There was no choice.'

'Of course there was a choice.' Jeremy sounded annoyed now. 'The first rule for rescue personnel is not to put themselves in danger.'

'You weren't there, Jeremy,' Penelope said wearily. 'You have absolutely no idea.' She caught Mark's gaze. 'If you're not too tired, I'd be very happy for you to stitch my arm.'

Jeremy's pager sounded as Belinda unwound the bandage from Penelope's arm and removed the dressing. Mark was donning sterile gloves and Jack was waiting with a swab and a bowl of antiseptic.

'You'll need a tetanus booster,' Matt said helpfully. 'I'll get it.'

'No!' Penelope was eyeing the syringe of local anaesthetic Belinda was now drawing up. One needle would be more than enough. 'I've had a tetanus shot in the last couple of years. They last for at least a decade.'

'You should still have a booster.'

Jeremy put down the telephone. 'I've got to get back to Theatre.' He peered at the cut on Penelope's arm. 'Looks nice and clean, anyway.'

'A soak in sea water's always good.' Penelope was still watching Belinda. It looked like a large amount of local.

'Let me buy you a drink later, Penny.' Jeremy stepped closer. 'To toast your success.'

'We're all going over to The Hovel,' Belinda told him. 'To toast *both* our superstars.' She winked at Penelope, clearly pleased that she could forward Plan B so casually. 'Maybe we'll see you there, Jeremy.'

'I'm sure you will.' Jeremy glanced at Mark. 'Make sure you do a good job.'

Mark's gaze was quizzical. He waited until Jeremy left Resus 2 and then leaned closer to Penelope. 'He seems to have a rather personal interest in my performance here. Is there something going on that I should know about?'

'No.' Penelope's answer was quick. She hoped it

hadn't been too hurried. 'Absolutely not,' she added. She couldn't help glancing at Belinda, whose face was a picture of innocence. Mark also glanced at Belinda. He looked momentarily puzzled but then his face settled into a professional neutrality.

'Let's get on with this,' he suggested. He picked up the syringe of local. 'I'm rather looking forward to putting my feet up and having a shot of something very warming. Like a whisky, perhaps.'

'Don't mention shots.' Penelope closed her eyes. 'Did I warn you that I'm a complete wimp?'

'I wouldn't have believed you, anyway.' Mark sounded as though he was smiling. 'I saw you doing your heroine bit, remember?'

'It all seems like a bad dream now.' Penelope kept her eyes firmly shut as she felt the sting of the needle. 'Especially this bit.'

'Sorry.' Mark was easing the needle further under her skin, numbing the edges of the cut. 'That's the worst bit over with. You can open your eyes now if you like.'

One by one, the extra staff members in Resus 2 were called away to other patients. By the time Mark had deftly looped the ends of the third suture and tied the knot they were alone and Penelope was watching the task closely. Mark was concentrating on what he was doing and seemed unaware of her gaze. She admired the confident movements of his hands as they manipulated the needle holder and scissors. Despite the masculine proportions of his hands, his touch on the instruments was delicate. The odd sensation this thought gave Penelope prompted her to transfer her gaze to Mark's face.

Absorbed by his task, Mark was unaware of the scrutiny. Penelope noted the intensity of his concentration and gathered the impression of a perfectionist at work. Someone who was determined to perform to the best of his ability and succeed due to a combination of intelligence and sensitivity. Penelope already knew that Mark had more than a fair measure of strength and courage to go with his other attributes. He really was quite an extraordinary man.

Penelope pulled her gaze away from Mark's face back to his hands. As he pushed the needle through one side of the cut he steadied his hand by resting its heel on Penelope's arm. The touch of skin against skin sent an unexpected physical reaction rocketing through Penelope. It was strong enough to make her catch her breath. Mark glanced up quickly.

'Did that hurt? Have I missed a spot with the local?'

'No—it's fine. Keep going.' Penelope kept her gaze averted. She didn't dare look at Mark in case he could read in her face what she had just felt. She needed a little time to try and analyse it herself first. She had never felt such a strong wave of physical attraction to anybody. Maybe it could be attributed to her state of exhaustion. If so, she would have to tire herself out a little more often. Penelope took a deep, slow breath. She had considered herself strongly attracted to Jeremy because of the tingling sensation she associated with physical desire. What she had just experienced thanks to the touch of Mark Wallace's hand hadn't been a tingle. It had been more like a lightning bolt.

The fifth suture was now in place. The job so far was impressively neat.

'You're very good at this,' Penelope told Mark.

'I've had plenty of practice.' Mark picked up a fresh suture needle. 'Another two and we should be done.' He smiled as Penelope yawned. 'Keeping you up, am I? You're probably far too tired to go any-where for a drink.'

'Bindy's giving me a ride home so I'll be going where she goes.' Penelope shook her head. 'I'm hardly dressed for an outing, though.'

'You look great.' Mark grinned. 'And so do I. I think we'll set a new fashion trend. Besides...' He paused, the new suture held in the air between them. 'I want to buy you a drink myself. It's the least I can do to resurrect the remnants of our date.'

'We never got anywhere near that house. I wonder what it was like?'

'I rang the owner while you were still in the shower and explained why we didn't show up. He's away for a few days but I've made another appoint-ment for next week.' Mark had put the needle through one side of the cut as he'd spoken. He inserted it carefully into the other side and drew the edges together. 'Would you like to try again and come with me?'

'Sure.' Penelope's eyes were drifting relentlessly shut. Her exhaustion could no longer be ignored. She was only dimly aware of the application of a new dressing on her arm and blankets being draped over her. The quiet voice was Mark's. Who was he talking to?

'She needs to go home and have a good sleep. She's not going anywhere for a drink tonight.'

'I can see that.' It was Belinda who had returned to Resus 2. Penelope tried to open her eyes and failed. 'I'll let her sleep here until I finish my shift and then I'll take her home.'

When Penelope awoke she found herself in her own bed with no clear memory of how she came to be there. It took a few moments to absorb the fact that she was wearing unusual sleeping attire and then the memory of how and why she came to be wearing a theatre scrub suit flooded back. The dull ache in her arm pushed any remaining fatigue further away. A glance at her bedside clock showed it to be early. Six a.m. Penelope could hear Belinda moving around the flat, getting ready to go to work. She climbed gingerly out of bed. Despite being stiff and sore, Penelope wanted to see her flatmate and find out how she had come to be in her own bed.

Belinda was delighted to see Penelope up. 'You've been asleep for nearly twelve hours. I was going to have to check your Glasgow coma score before I left.'

'I'm alert.' Penelope smiled. 'Sort of. How on earth did I get home? I really can't remember.'

'I'm not surprised. You were practically comatose,' Belinda informed her. 'I parked in the ambulance bay and Mark carried you out to my car.' She dropped teabags into two mugs and added boiling water. 'Jeremy was in the department after intubating a cerebrovascular accident that came in while you were snoring in Resus 2. You should have seen his face.' Belinda sighed with satisfaction as she added milk to the mugs of tea. 'This plan is working perfectly.'

'Plan? What plan?' Penelope rubbed her eyes. Maybe it was an overdose of sleep that robbed Belinda's statement of any clear meaning.

'The plan to make Jeremy jealous,' Belinda reminded her. 'It's working perfectly. He thinks you and Mark are heading off to save the planet together and he's not going to let you escape. The slightest nod from you now, girl, and he'll be *exactly* where you want him to be.'

'I don't want him to be anywhere.' Penelope accepted the mug of tea. Her thought processes were clearing rapidly. 'Plan B is cancelled, Bindy. It doesn't exist. It's history.'

'What?' Belinda's jaw dropped. 'What about those four kids that need to get to school before you turn forty? The ones that Jeremy was going to father for you.'

'Jeremy Lane is history,' Penelope told her calmly. 'I'm not interested any more.'

'Why not?' Belinda shook her head. 'You've spent weeks panting for him to notice you. Now he has and you've changed your mind.' She whistled silently. 'Even I don't tease men like that, Pen.'

'I'm not teasing anybody,' Penelope said defensively. 'I've just come to my senses. Realised what's really important.'

'Is this because of your near death by drowning experience?'

'Kind of.' Penelope sipped her tea carefully. She didn't want to tell Belinda how she felt about Mark. Not yet, anyway. The feeling was too new. Too fragile. And it might not come to anything. The only sure knowledge she had right now was that Jeremy was not the man she wanted. Compared to Mark, he just didn't make the grade any more and Penelope would rather be alone than settle for second best.

Belinda sighed, conceding that she wasn't going to get Penelope to talk about the subject any further for the moment.

'I'd better get going. I'll see you when I get home after three.'

'You'll see me before then. I start at twelve.'

'You're not planning to go in to work today? You're supposed to stay home and recuperate.'

'I don't need to.'

'But your arm!'

'My arm's fine. It's well covered and it's not going to get in the way of me working.' Penelope tried to sound firm. She wanted to go in to work today. How else would she even have the possibility of seeing Mark? A sore arm and a few aches and pains elsewhere were certainly not enough of a reason to stay home. 'I've practically slept the clock around,' she reminded Belinda. 'I'll go back to bed for an hour or two now and then I'll have a quiet morning. I might drop in on Rachael at the clinic and see if she's got time for a coffee.'

Belinda sighed again. 'You're stubborn, Penelope Baker. It's a shame you can't apply the same determination to sorting out your love life.'

'But I have.'

Belinda shook her head. 'No, you haven't. You've gone off Plan B and you won't even tell me why. How can I help you if I don't know what's going on?' She turned her gaze to her wristwatch. 'Oh, help. I'm going to be late. Say hi to Rachael for me when you see her. It's been way too long.'

* * *

'It's been way too long, Penny.'

'I know. I'm sorry.'

'I was beginning to wonder if I was going to see you or this baby first.'

'You're only five months pregnant, Rache.' Penelope smiled fondly at her younger sister. 'Though I must say you're looking a lot fatter than the last time I saw you.'

'I probably wasn't pregnant then.' Rachael returned the smile. 'It's been months.'

'Weeks,' Penelope corrected. 'And if you're going to keep giving me a hard time I'll go away again.'

'Sorry.' Rachael settled back in the armchair. 'It's just that I've missed you and you pick a day to drop in when I've got fourteen cats to spay for the SPCA and a Bichon coming in for a Caesarean at eleven-thirty. I've only got time for half a cup of tea as it is.'

'I'll come around for dinner soon. You can show me the pink bunnies you're painting on the nursery walls.'

'Bunnies!' Rachael looked horrified. 'Yin and Yang symbols, more likely.' She pushed her long blonde braid back over her shoulder. 'You're put off by this baby business, aren't you? I've been too much of a bore, talking about nothing else, and you're not interested. I'm sorry, Pen. Of course it's boring for you.'

'It's not boring. I'm really excited for you about this baby, Rache. I know just how you feel and I wouldn't expect you to talk about anything else. I'm just...I'm just a bit envious, I guess.'

'What about?' Rachael looked astonished.

'You're three years younger than me,' Penelope reminded her sister. 'And you've got all the things I'd love to have. An interesting career you can still do when you've got children. Your own house with a lovely garden. A husband who adores you and now a baby on the way. It's perfect.'

'Hardly.' Rachael grinned. 'Try spaying fourteen cats in a row and see how interesting you think my career is.' She bit her lip. 'I thought that might be part of it. I know how Mum goes on and on about her grandchildren and how it's time for you to settle down and contribute to the numbers. Just ignore her.'

'It's not that easy. Especially when it's what I want myself.'

'It'll happen. The right man is out there.' Rachael smiled at Penelope reassuringly. 'I'll bet he's not even very far away.'

'I'm not holding my breath,' Penelope said lightly. 'Not with my history of disasters. But I shouldn't let it come between us. I'm going to enjoy being an aunt again and I'm especially looking forward to it this time. I'll be able to spend as much time with your baby as I like and then hand it back if it cries too much or needs a nappy change.' Penelope smiled. 'I'm just sorry we didn't talk about it before. I feel better now. You'll be seeing a lot more of me from now on and we can talk babies all you like.'

'Boring,' Rachael declared. 'I want to hear more about this rescue yesterday. How come your picture wasn't in the newspaper today?' She reached for the paper lying on the Formica table of the veterinary clinic's small staffroom. 'Who's this guy?'

'Mark Wallace. A new registrar. He did most of the heroic stuff. I just helped.'

'Hmm. So how did you slice your arm, then?'

'Crawling inside the car, I guess.' Penelope grinned. 'I'll tell you all about it. I'll check my roster as soon as I get into work this afternoon and ring you to organise a night for dinner.'

'Bring Bindy, too, if she's off. We haven't seen her for ages either.' Rachael was still inspecting the newspaper picture. 'He's cute,' she pronounced. 'What were you doing out with him?' She eyed Penelope. 'Is he part of why I haven't been seeing you?'

'No.' Penelope shook her head. 'It wasn't a date.' She paused and then caught Rachael's sceptical gaze and smiled. 'Kind of close to a date, I guess.'

'Aha!' Rachael looked delighted. 'About time, too. You've been waiting long enough for him to ask you out.'

'No, that was someone else,' Penelope confessed. 'I'm not remotely interested in *him* any more.'

Rachael's eyes widened. 'There must be something pretty special about this new man, then.'

Penelope hesitated. Her smile faded and her nod was serious. 'I think there is. I get the feeling that there's definitely something very special about him. I guess time will tell.'

'Maybe this time it's it,' Rachael suggested. 'I hope so, Pen.'

'So do I, Rache,' Penelope said softly. 'So do I.'

CHAPTER FIVE

THE pain on trying to move was an unpleasant surprise.

Mark groaned aloud as he eased himself carefully into a sitting position on the edge of his bed. Every muscle in his body was protesting and some of the twinges were sharp enough to make him wonder if he'd done himself some real damage. It took several, very slow minutes for Mark to persuade his body that a move into a hot shower could be beneficial. The warmth was certainly comforting but his determination to make the 3 p.m. start to his shift in Emergency was still being undermined.

A few anti-inflammatories, part of his brain advised. Another few hours in bed. Nobody really expects you to turn up for work today. Jack said there'd be no problem arranging cover. Mark reached for the soap. No wonder he felt as sore as he did. Some of the bruises he'd collected were quite impressive—especially the one on his right thigh. His right knee was rather swollen as well but he couldn't remember any specific knock that might have been responsible. Maybe he'd twisted the joint when he'd found himself caught in the back seat of the submerged car, trying so desperately to unfasten the clips that were pinning the baby in its car seat.

Mark sucked in his breath as the soap made contact with the large abrasion on his left upper arm but the superficial discomfort was easy enough to dismiss. It was all pretty superficial, in fact. He hadn't even needed stitches. Unlike Penny. Mark turned off the shower and stepped out, ignoring the twinge in his back as he reached for a towel. Of course he was going in to work today. Even if Penny didn't make it in, he could find out how she was from Belinda or someone else. Maybe he could find out her telephone number and talk to her himself. Mark towelled himself more vigorously. The pain was definitely abating now. Yes. He had every intention of talking to Penny himself. As often as possible.

Life was really an astonishing business sometimes. Mark wrapped the towel around his waist and rubbed the condensation off the bathroom mirror so he could see himself shaving. The fact that a change of job would throw him into a whole new network of people had been one of the reasons he'd chosen to move. That some of those people would be female and attractive was only to be expected. A bonus that Mark had intended to appreciate—at a safe distance. At the ripe age of thirty-six Mark was now mature enough to recognise the danger of getting closer. Hell, if Joanna had taught him nothing else, she had driven that particular lesson home with painful clarity.

What Mark hadn't expected was Penelope Baker. Mark shook his head in disbelief as he rinsed his razor. He probably wouldn't have even put her on the top of any list of attractive women in the department. Especially when she was in the company of that stunning redhead, her friend Belinda. Or—Mark found himself grinning—when she'd just had a long shower and had scrubbed pink cheeks and wildly fluffy hair. He'd appreciated the friendly gesture of the offer to drive him to see the house, however, and Penelope had been easy to talk to. Pleasant company. Mark didn't know anybody in Wellington yet and friendly gestures ought to be encouraged. He hadn't really been serious in calling the outing a date, had he? It was difficult to remember now because his feelings towards Penelope had undergone a rather radical change during the course of that dramatic afternoon.

She'd blown him away with her demonstration of determination and courage in dealing with the disaster. No hint of panic. She'd dealt with the resuscitation of that baby with calm competence. Saved its life, in fact, and that hadn't been enough for her. She'd disobeyed his instructions and dived into the wreck when she must have been just as aware of the danger as he'd been. And probably just as terrified. Penelope had courage all right. Hadn't even flinched when he'd sewn up her arm, and that couldn't have been pleasant. She'd been watching the procedure, too. The memory of catching the gaze from those astonishingly dark blue eyes gave Mark a very odd sensation in his gut.

Cupping his hands under the running cold water to splash the remains of shaving foam from his face, Mark acknowledged that it was the same sensation he'd had when he'd carried Penelope out to Bindy's car yesterday. A desire to protect her, perhaps. Mark turned the tap off firmly. A desire, full stop, he warned himself. For heaven's sake, had the lesson learned from Joanna worn off already? Maybe he should take the day off. Go back to bed and spend the time constructively reminding himself that he was never, ever going to set himself up for that kind of pain again.

St Margaret's emergency department was humming. Mark couldn't believe the chaos he stepped into a few minutes before 3 p.m. The department was completely clogged with people, including an extraordinary number of small children. The cubicles were all occupied and the curtains pulled around all resus areas indicated their use. Beds were lining the sides of the central corridor and three ambulance stretchers containing patients were queued at the sorting desk.

What space was left seemed to be filled with yet

more people. Some were adults who were standing around looking vaguely bewildered. Some were staff members who looked flustered—standing still only long enough to gather equipment or answer queries. Most were children and many of them weren't standing still at all. Three small boys rushed past Mark as he stopped in amazement to survey the scene. One of the boys tripped over his foot.

'Careful!' Mark picked the boy up. 'Where's your mother?'

'Dunno.' The boy gave Mark a suspicious look and then wriggled free of his grasp. 'Hey, Brendon! Wait for me!'

The child took off and barrelled into the nurse coming towards him. He found his arm firmly caught.

'Timmy. Didn't I tell you to stay sitting with the others?' Penelope sounded annoyed.

'Yeah, but Brendon and Jamie went to find Miss Rogers. I wanted to go with them.'

'Well, you can't.' Penelope was still holding the boy's arm. 'Where are Brendon and Jamie now?'

Mark was grinning. 'I think that might be them helping themselves to syringes from the IV trolley.'

Penelope's smile at noticing Mark faded by the time he had finished speaking. 'I don't believe this,' she groaned.

'Neither do I. What's going on?'

'School picnic. Half of them came down with

food poisoning and the other half had to come in as well. The waiting room's overflowing and the ones that aren't sick keep escaping.' Penelope was pulling Timmy along beside her. 'Brendon! Jamie! Put those back right now.'

The curtain from Resus 3 opened and Jack appeared. 'Ah, Mark. Thank goodness. How are you?'

'Fine, thanks.' This was no time to pass on any minor personal complaints. 'Where do you need me?'

Jack cast an eye around the department. 'Chaos, isn't it? The nursing staff are trying to cope with the children and we've got extra staff on the way. We've got a multi-system trauma that's tied up half the doctors. We've also got three chest pains, two acute abdos, and a drug overdose. Belinda's on triage. She'll direct you to the patients that need urgent attention.'

Penelope now had the three small boys in tow. 'You have to come back to the waiting room,' she told them. 'Didn't you see the toys in there?'

'I don't feel well,' Timmy responded. He dragged Penelope to a halt as they passed Resus 1. Timmy's face emptied of colour in a dramatic fashion.

'Oh, no!' Penelope cast a wild gaze around her, probably hoping to spot a vomit container. The nearest pile was on the end of the sorting desk and Penelope made a lunge for the small plastic bucket, but she was too late by about three seconds.

Brendon and Jamie eyed the mess on the floor with admiration.

'Man! That really stinks,' Brendon informed Timmy.

A nurse aide was already moving towards them, a bucket and mop in her hand and a resigned expression on her face. Belinda put down the telephone at the sorting desk and also made a move.

'They're clearing the paediatric observation unit upstairs,' she told Jack. 'We can start moving some children in that direction.'

'Have we got a head count yet?'

'There were forty-eight children and fourteen adults on the picnic. Sounds like the barbecued chicken was the culprit. Most of them have eaten it but only half of them are sick so far.'

Penelope was wiping a very subdued Timmy's face with a damp cloth. Brendon and Jamie had vanished again. A woman pushed past the ambulance stretchers, having gained entrance from the loading bay.

'Where's my daughter? I just heard she's terribly sick.'

'Mark, there's a possible anterior infarction in Resus 1. She's been here for ten minutes.'

'I'm on my way.' Mark touched Penelope's shoulder as he squeezed through the expanding knot of people around the sorting desk. 'Are you OK, Pen?'

'Her name's Bridie. Bridie Pearson,' the woman told Belinda tearfully. 'Where is she?'

Penelope caught Mark's eye and her strained expression softened noticeably. 'I will be,' she answered his query, 'if we survive this lot. I'll catch you later.'

Mark smiled. 'Don't worry, you'll survive. You're a heroine.' He disappeared behind the curtain screening Resus 1.

'I feel better now,' Timmy announced. 'Can I go and play with Brendon and Jamie again? Where are they?'

'Heaven only knows,' Penelope muttered. 'Let's go and find them.'

Over the next hour the emergency department underwent one of the total transformations in atmosphere that made it such an interesting place to work. From a state of chaos that stretched its staff apparently beyond their capabilities it became a demonstration of focused management plans going into action. Patients were treated and transferred. Relatives were directed to family members and kept informed. Nursing staff followed treatment protocols, assisted doctors in their assessments and did their best to keep up with documentation. Telephones rang constantly and auxiliary staff came and went in large numbers.

Another hour slipped past and magically the department entered one of its periodic lulls. The staff gratefully grabbed the opportunity to collect themselves and the staffroom was crowded—coffee and laughter being shared in equal quantities.

'I'm never touching chicken again at a barbecue. That poor young teacher—Miss Rogers. Did you ever see anyone throwing up that violently?'

'Don't go into the waiting room. It'll take a week to get the smell out.'

'Who were those two little monsters having the water fight with syringes?'

'Brendon and Jamie.' Penelope groaned, coming into the room in time to hear the query. 'I was supposed to be looking after them.'

Penelope was ushered to a seat at the table by Matt.

'You look even worse than I feel,' someone told her.

'You shouldn't even be at work today, Penny,' Matt said. 'You do look terrible.'

'Gee, thanks.'

'I told her to stay home.' Belinda put her mug of coffee down with a bump. 'But do you think she'd listen? No.' Belinda answered her own question with a grin. 'She just had to be a martyr and come to work.'

'She certainly knew what day to pick, didn't she?'

'Must be bad karma,' someone else suggested.

'What dreadful things did you do in a past life, Penny?'

'She just couldn't stay away from us,' Matt put in. 'Our company is just too good to miss.'

Penelope knew that Mark had entered the room even before she could see him. Her eyes were drawn instantly to the bench where he was making a cup of coffee. Had he been looking for her in the crowded room or was it coincidence that their gazes caught so quickly? She could feel herself blushing. Would Mark guess that the only reason she hadn't taken the day off to recuperate had been because it was his company that was too good to miss?

'I'm fine,' Penelope declared. 'Just a bit tired.' Mark was closer to the table now. 'Nice photo of you in the paper, Mark. Was that Tommy's father holding him?'

Mark nodded. 'You should have been in the photo as well.' He smiled. 'Unfortunately you were comatose in Resus 2. We didn't want to wake you up.'

'Thank goodness for that.' Penelope could remember how her hair had looked. 'How's Tommy's mother doing, do you know?'

'She's fine. I went up to see her before I came on duty. She'll be going home today or tomorrow. Tommy went home with his dad last night.'

'What were you two doing on the Shelly Bay road, anyway?' Matt asked. 'Is this something we should know about?'

'Not at all,' Mark said nonchalantly. 'I'm hunting for a house to rent. Penny kindly saved me the trouble of renting a car.'

'Oh, yeah!' The general comment was knowing and Penelope's blush returned.

'You're a fast mover, Mark Wallace,' a nurse aide observed. 'You've only been here for a week.'

Mark's glance at Penelope was apologetic. It acknowledged the downside of working in an environment with large staff numbers who worked closely together. The ability to generate and spread rumours was legend. All hospitals were the same and Penelope's smile said she wasn't bothered. The ghost of a wink that Belinda gave her friend suggested that if she hadn't really given up on Plan B, the generation of a rumour was an excellent development and its spread should be encouraged. Especially if the spread included the department of anaesthetics.

Penelope finished her coffee. 'I've got a patient I'd better get back to,' she announced. She gave Belinda an imperceptible shake of her head. She didn't want Jeremy persuaded that she was a desirable prize. She was regretting ever confiding in Belinda that she had been attracted to the man. That attraction hadn't been the real thing at all. She'd had no idea what the real thing was until she'd met Mark. Penelope would have to tell Belinda the truth very soon. As soon as she knew whether there was any chance of what she felt for Mark being explored any further.

The opportunity for gaining that knowledge didn't arrive until the following week. Mark had purchased his own car by then but he still seemed keen that Penelope accompany him to see the house, which turned out to be perfect. It wasn't too large and it was old enough to have real character. The house was perched on a steep slope. French doors from a small living room opened onto a deck supported by stilts as it jutted out into mid-air. Any view of the road beneath was obscured by the wooden platform and the native trees in the garden below. It felt rather like they were standing right over the surf that boiled onto large rocks on the foreshore.

'This will be fantastic on a hot day in summer.'

'Mmm.' Mark smiled at Penelope's enthusiasm. 'All three of them.'

'It's not that bad,' the owner of the house assured Mark. 'I've spent a lot of time out here, getting a tan.'

'Don't worry. I love it,' Mark responded. 'Even the worst weather won't put me off. That fireplace in the living room is magnificent.'

'There's a woodshed out the back.' The owner nodded. 'Probably enough wood in there to last you a season.'

Even with the French doors closed again behind them, the crash of the surf could be clearly heard. Scorching Bay was on the other side of the peninsula that formed part of Wellington's harbour. The surf here could be as wild as any stretch of open coastline. It would be dramatic in a storm but right now the sound was soothing. Penelope could imagine the pleasure of lying in bed, going to sleep, lulled by that background rhythm. Her imagination took another leap. Any bed in this house would contain Mark. The imagined pleasure now had nothing whatsoever to do with the sound of the sea.

'What do you think, Pen?'

Penelope tried to marshal her errant thoughts, carefully avoiding any eye contact with Mark. 'Ah…' She stared at the stonework framing the huge fireplace. Taking a deep breath, she turned and smiled at Mark. 'I think it's fantastic. You should move in as soon as you can.'

'I will.' Mark stretched his hand towards the owner of the house to shake hands on the deal. 'Thanks. How soon *can* I move in?'

'I'll be gone in two weeks. You realise that the place will be completely unfurnished, don't you?'

'No problem. That gives me plenty of time to hunt for some furniture.' He grinned at Penelope. 'I might even be able to enlist a bit of assistance.'

'Sure.' Penelope was happy to confirm her availability for the mission. 'Any time.'

Any time wasn't nearly soon enough. Work schedules threatened to seriously undermine Penelope's quest for information regarding Mark's interest in her. Their rosters seemed to go through a period of mismatching so that whenever Penelope was working, Mark was having time off. The only real bonus over the next few days was that Mark took the stitches out of her arm. It was a quiet moment together that led to an invitation for a drink after work. The downside was that they weren't alone in consuming the drink. The postponement of the congratulatory celebration of the heroic efforts surrounding the rescue of Kerry and her baby over a week ago had not been forgotten and it seemed that half the emergency department decided to join them at the pub after Penelope had told Belinda where she and Mark were going.

The other unwelcome development was the dinner invitation from Jeremy. After all this time he had finally asked her for a date and Penelope was relieved to discover that she wasn't remotely interested. Even so, it proved difficult to refuse politely.

'I can't, I'm sorry, Jeremy. I'm working.'

'Another time, then.'

'Um…. No, I don't think so. Sorry.' Penelope gave Jeremy the briefest of glances, still trying to maintain a level of courtesy. 'But thanks for asking.' Penelope felt even more uncomfortable after catching the blatant interest in Jeremy's gaze. 'I've got to go. I've got a patient waiting for me.' Her smile was forced. Surely Jeremy had gained a clear message by now. She couldn't have been too rude because the anaesthetic registrar didn't appear bothered.

'Sure, Penny. Catch you later.'

The worst thing was that Mark had witnessed the exchange. Penelope attempted a nonchalant smile but had the distinct impression that it was a failure. Mark's expression was quizzical even from a distance and he turned away without returning her smile. Penelope spent an anxious night wondering what he might be thinking, but she was reassured the following day when Mark found her at the sorting desk. He wasn't actually due to start his shift until after Penelope finished hers in twenty minutes. It seemed as though he had come in early with the intention of catching her.

'I've been checking the roster and we both have a day off tomorrow. How would you feel about helping me hunt for some furniture? I'm due to move into that house next week so I'm running out of time.'

'I'd love to,' Penelope said happily. He had come in early to catch her. And he wanted her company. He had a lot of furniture to find as well. It could take a long time.

'I'll pick you up about ten,' Mark offered.

'OK.'

There was a pause. 'You'd better let me have your address, then,' Mark suggested with a smile.

Penelope laughed. 'Could be useful, I guess.'

'And your phone number. Just in case something unexpected crops up.'

'OK.' Penelope scribbled down the details and handed the scrap of paper to Mark. They could have met at the hospital or The Hovel. She was delighted to be asked to provide something this personal. 'Ten o'clock, then.'

'I'll be looking forward to it.'

'Me, too.'

It turned out that Mark didn't like modern furniture, which suited Penelope just fine. She much preferred exploring secondhand or antique shops.

'I know,' she exclaimed during their discussion of where to go first. 'There's a huge warehouse shop on the coast road at Paraparaumu. It's a bit of a drive to get there but they have wonderful stuff and it's all old.'

'Sounds brilliant. We've got the time and it's a lovely day for a drive up the coast.'

The antique warehouse was well north of the city, situated off the main coastal road, a stone's throw from the Paraparaumu beach. The oversized stable doors that formed the entrance to the vast building were flanked by ancient farm wagons. The rusting iron wheels wouldn't be turning again in any hurry.

A young man with short dreadlocked hair and a T-shirt bearing the shop's logo was arranging tubs of vivid orange and yellow marigolds around the wagon wheels.

'Hi. Are you guys looking for anything in particular?'

'Everything,' Mark responded. 'I need to furnish a whole house.'

'Excellent! You've come to the right place. We deliver stuff as well.'

'Great. I'll bear that in mind.'

'You want help? I can navigate for you. It's kind of big in there. I'm Shane, by the way.'

'I think we'll cope, thanks, Shane.' Mark was moving towards the doors. 'I've got all day and I've brought my interior design consultant.'

Shane grinned at Penelope. 'Sounds like a cool job. Does it pay well?'

'No, and the hours are lousy.'

'Come on.' Mark was waiting by the entrance. 'We've got some serious hunting to do here.'

'The clients can be very bossy as well,' Penelope told Shane. 'I'll be lucky if I'm even allowed to stop for lunch.'

'I'll give you lunch,' Mark promised. 'After you've earned it. Come on, woman.'

Penelope rolled her eyes at the sales assistant. 'See what I mean?'

Shane laughed. 'There's a great fish and chip shop down the road. Just before you hit the beach.'

The thought of the fish and chip shop was becoming decidedly attractive as the grandfather clock at the bottom of a staircase chimed twice.

'Good grief! We've been here for nearly three hours,' Penelope exclaimed. She flopped down on an oversized and distinctly battered leather couch that happened to be beside them.

'Don't give up yet,' Mark pleaded. He sat down beside her on the vast couch. 'We've been doing so well. This place is a treasure trove.'

Penelope held up her hand with her fingers splayed. 'You've got a kitchen table and six chairs. Four huge bookshelves and a coffee-table.' She was counting the items on her fingers. 'You've also got a Scotch chest, a wardrobe and a totally useless hat stand.'

'Not useless,' Mark protested. 'It's for coats as well.'

'It's huge. The house is small.' Penelope thought about the stand again. It was a solid piece of old Kauri furniture with a large mirror set beneath a row of hooks and a bench seat with space for overshoes at its base. Even the sides were solid panels of carved wood. It would weigh a ton.

'It's got an umbrella stand on the side,' Mark reminded her cunningly. 'With a tin tray to catch the drips.'

Penelope laughed. 'That could be useful,' she conceded. 'Have you got an umbrella?'

'Not yet. I'm sure there'll be one around here somewhere, though. They've got everything.'

'You've got everything you need. I want some lunch.'

'Soon,' Mark promised. 'I haven't got any crockery yet. Or pots. Or linen.'

'You don't want antique linen,' Penelope said firmly. 'You can go into the city and find a department store. Another day.'

'I haven't got a bed.'

'Oh.' Penelope tried to ignore the attractive mental juxtaposition of Mark and a bed that sprang instantly to mind. The effort was enough to send a flush of colour to her cheeks and make it difficult to say anything before the moment had stretched into significance. 'I guess you will need one,' Penelope said hurriedly. She tried to sound businesslike. 'What size did you want? Single? Double? Queen?'

'Definitely not a single,' Mark murmured. He had his eyes shut. 'Far too small.'

'Oh.' Now Penelope could imagine Mark in a big bed. Big enough for someone else to share. She stole a glance at the man beside her. His legs were encased in soft-looking faded denim. The broad shoulders were covered in a woollen pullover that looked equally soft and comfortable. Mark's eyes were still shut, dark lashes against his cheeks and a stray wave of matching hair flopping onto his forehead. Penelope had to resist the urge to brush it back into place. She pulled her gaze further down his face. Mark's lips were curved slightly into a contented smile. Even they looked soft. Inviting... Oh, help! Penelope stood up.

'Come on, then,' she ordered briskly. 'We'll find you a bed and then I want lunch or I'll resign as your interior design consultant. I can tell you now, you won't find someone else for the job. Not with working conditions like this.'

Mark opened his eyes and smiled directly at Penelope. 'I like this couch.'

'It's scruffy.'

'It's very comfortable. I can just imagine it calling me after a hard day's work. We'll put it in front of a roaring fire and sit and listen to the rain beating on the tin roof.'

Penelope returned the smile a little tentatively. 'We'? Was she going to be sitting on the scruffy but very comfortable couch in front of the fire as well?

'OK. You can have the couch. Let's find a bed before I die of starvation.'

Mark's eyebrows shot up. 'Wow! You can be kind of direct when you want to be.' He jumped to his feet. 'Not that I'm complaining, mind you. I like decisive women. A bed we shall find. Forthwith.'

Penelope ignored the innuendo. She waved at

Shane who was observing them from a central desk area. He came towards them quickly.

'We need a bed,' Penelope told him crisply.

'Yeah?' Shane winked at Mark. 'Of course you do.' He pointed ahead of them. 'Come right this way. The beds are over there past the bathroom fittings.'

Penelope sighed as she kept her gaze on the claw-foot baths they walked past. Had Mark stopped grinning at Shane yet? He could choose this bed by himself. If he suggested testing an old mattress he would be right out of luck. This game was getting a little too personal for comfort.

'Look, Pen!' Mark caught hold of her elbow. 'That's perfect, don't you think?'

Penelope looked. The double brass bed ends had seen better days. The black paint was chipped in places and the brass knobs were dull. They could easily be polished, however, and the porcelain flower inserts were lovely.

'It doesn't have a mattress,' Shane pointed out. 'But it's standard double size so it won't be hard to find one. We've got heaps.'

'I'll get a new mattress, thanks,' Mark told him.

'Good thinking. The old ones always sag.' Shane shook his dreadlocks. 'Bad for your back.'

Penelope looked around her. Surely there was something that would catch her interest enough to distract her from thinking about sharing a mattress with Mark Wallace. He seemed to require distraction himself.

'Right. That's it. I've made a list. I'll pay for everything now and arrange a delivery date.' Mark grinned at Shane. 'If I don't provide lunch now I suspect I'll get fired.'

'I thought you were the boss.'

'Appearances can be deceptive.' Mark was opening his cheque-book. 'Where did you say the fish and chip shop was?'

The shop lived up to its reputation. The food was great. Mark and Penelope ate the freshly battered and perfectly cooked fish fillets sitting on a bench outside. The warmth of the sunshine and the sight of the beach beside them were too inviting to ignore.

'Fancy walking off lunch?' Mark queried.

'Sounds good to me.'

Penelope rolled up the legs of her jeans and removed her sandals. Mark followed suit. Within a couple of minutes they were walking barefoot on the sand, their footwear dangling in their hands. Unusually subdued surf sent gentle waves rolling onto the impressive expanse of soft, golden sand. Sunlight caught the foaming finale of the waves, making them glisten seductively. By tacit consent, Penelope and Mark walked closer to the surf until sea water washed over their bare feet.

'This water is freezing,' Mark exclaimed. 'People don't swim here, do they?'

'Of course. It'll warm up quite a lot after Christmas.' Penelope grinned as another small wave caught their ankles. 'It *is* a bit chilly, isn't it?'

'Arctic. As cold as the harbour.'

'No. Nothing's that cold.' The memory made Penelope shudder. 'I thought I'd never get warm again.'

'You and me both.'

Mark caught Penelope's hand in a friendly gesture of agreement. They continued the walk both lost for a moment in their memories of that grim afternoon. At least, Penelope was. Mark's thoughts had turned in an entirely new direction thanks to the pressure of Penelope's hand holding his. It couldn't hurt to take this a bit further, could it? Penelope had seemed uncomfortable in the warehouse when the search had centred on finding a bed. Had she guessed what he had been thinking? That any bed he might find could only be perfectly satisfactory if Penelope Baker would consent to share it with him—at least occasionally? He wanted to kiss this woman. He wanted to… Mark had to clear his throat. He gazed at the vast expanse of sand stretching before them. He just wanted, full stop, and the force of the wanting was causing a distinctly physical discomfort.

Penelope was aware of the warmth of the firm grip on her hand that Mark seemed in no hurry to relinquish. She could feel the warmth of the sun caressing her back. The periodic chill of the sea water at her feet only accentuated the pleasure of the warmth. The feeling of companionship was also a pleasure. In fact, Penelope couldn't remember ever feeling happier than she had in the last few hours. The fun of furniture shopping with Mark. The excitement that the innuendoes of physical attraction had given her. The contentment of sharing a meal together and now this walk on a sunny, deserted beach. They were completely alone. Together. It was...

'Arghh!' Penelope shrieked. 'Oh, *no*!'

The large wave had taken them both by complete surprise. It would have knocked her off her feet if Mark hadn't caught her around the waist. As it was, they were both saturated to thigh level and thoroughly splashed up to their shoulders. Mark held her close as the pull of the retreating wave threatened her balance again.

'I don't believe this!' Penelope clung to Mark. 'We're soaked!'

'Again,' Mark added. He was laughing. 'What is it about dates with you, Penelope Baker? Do you like getting wet or something?'

'What makes you so sure it's my fault?' Penelope was also laughing as she tilted her head to argue. 'I've never had this problem with men before.'

'Haven't you?' Mark had stopped laughing. His tone was as solemn as his gaze. 'Is it a problem, Pen?'

'No.' Penelope's response was soft. 'I don't think it is.'

The wave was long gone but Mark hadn't moved. He still held Penelope close with one arm. With his other hand he brushed damp curls away from her face.

'No,' he agreed softly. 'I don't think it is either.' His hand stayed on the side of her face as he bent his head to touch her lips gently with his own.

The shock of pleasure the touch sent through Penelope's entire body was enough to make her gasp. Mark's lips moved over hers and the questing touch of his tongue chased any conscious thought into the far distance. Penelope wound her arms around his neck, feeling Mark's fingers slide beneath her hair as he cradled her head and explored her mouth with exquisite thoroughness.

Penelope had no idea how many waves broke around their knees as they stood there. She wasn't even aware of how cold she was becoming until her shudder made Mark break their kisses and pull her body even closer to his.

'You're freezing,' he told her. 'I'm not going to be responsible for giving you hypothermia twice in as many weeks. Come on—I'm taking you home.'

Penelope responded a little reluctantly to the pull on her hand. Going home meant separating, and she wanted to stay with Mark.

'If you have a nice long soak in a hot bath when

you get home, it'll be nearly time for dinner,' Mark observed. 'Then I could come and pick you up and we could go out somewhere.'

Penelope gave a skip to catch up with Mark's long stride. 'Sounds great.'

'What, the bath?'

'And the dinner. What sort of food do you like?'

'Almost anything. You choose.' Mark smiled down at Penelope. 'Pen?'

'Mmm?' Penelope was thinking about the various ethnic restaurants she knew of. Ones that had a nice intimate atmosphere.

'Let's make a pact first.'

'OK.' Penelope was sure she'd be happy to agree to any pact Mark wanted to make with her. Especially one that might require a kiss to seal it. 'What sort of pact?'

'Let's stay warm. And keep our clothes dry for a change.'

'OK.' Penelope caught Mark's gaze. She raised her eyebrows. Did he know how pacts were supposed to be sealed? As he pulled her to a halt she bit her lip with anticipated delight.

Mark did know. And if the look in those dark green eyes was anything to judge by, this pact was going to be exceptionally well sealed.

CHAPTER SIX

IT WAS really quite ironic.

If Plan B had lasted more than a few brief hours, Jeremy would have been disinclined to co-operate at all. Penelope had never found acting to be one of her strengths and she could never have kept up a convincing performance if she had feigned any part of her relationship with Mark. Because Plan B was history—as was any interest in Jeremy—the anaesthetist would have deserved at least a Minor Academy award for the way he was playing his originally intended part.

At one time Penelope had found excuses to be in the same area of the emergency department as Jeremy as often as possible. Now Jeremy was finding excuses to be in the department as often as possible. He wanted to check on a patient or add something to the paperwork. He forgot things. Like on the following Wednesday morning, when he returned to claim his stethoscope—accidentally left in the trauma room.

Penelope had been busy with a young patient who had suffered extreme dizziness and then collapse from an unknown cause. The teenager's pulse had

NO POSTAGE
NECESSARY
IF MAILED
IN THE
UNITED STATES

BUSINESS REPLY MAIL
FIRST-CLASS MAIL   PERMIT NO. 717-003   BUFFALO, NY

POSTAGE WILL BE PAID BY ADDRESSEE

HARLEQUIN READER SERVICE
3010 WALDEN AVE
PO BOX 1867
BUFFALO NY 14240-9952

Get FREE BOOKS and a FREE GIFT when you play the...

LAS VEGAS GAME

Just scratch off the gold box with a coin. Then check below to see the gifts you get!

YES! I have scratched off the gold Box. Please send me my **2 FREE BOOKS** and **gift for which I qualify.** I understand that I am under no obligation to purchase any books as explained on the back of this card.

382 HDL DVCJ   182 HDL DVCP

FIRST NAME	LAST NAME

ADDRESS

APT.#	CITY

STATE/PROV.   ZIP/POSTAL CODE

(H-IB-12/03)

7	7	7	Worth TWO FREE BOOKS plus a BONUS Mystery Gift!
🍒	🍒	🍒	Worth TWO FREE BOOKS!
🔔	🔔	♣	TRY AGAIN!

felt irregular and Penelope collected the 12-lead ECG machine to take into Resus 3 with some urgency. If her patient was suffering from an arrhythmia that had been the cause of the loss of consciousness, then it could be serious enough to cause a cardiac arrest if it happened again. She had to push the heavy machine past Jeremy, who had stopped in the central corridor to talk to Jack.

'Richard Milne?' The anaesthetist was saying. 'I believe he got discharged from Orthopaedics last week after he got a weight-bearing cast on that leg with the fractured femur.'

'What about his neck? Did he get any complications from the cricothyroidectomy?'

'None at all. Took a few days for the swelling to resolve completely but... Good *morning*, Penny.' The pause and the smile were both heavily appreciative.

The change in tone was enough to make Jack's eyebrows rise perceptibly.

'Morning.' Penelope's eye contact with Jeremy was only just long enough to be courteous. She was grateful for the urgency of her mission and propelled the machine ahead without pause.

It was a surprise to find Jeremy still loitering in the department when she emerged from Resus 3 with the detailed recording of her patient's heart rhythm. It wasn't a pleasant surprise. Annoyingly, Jeremy was now talking to Mark as well. Penelope had to talk to Mark herself because he was due to see her patient. She approached the two doctors.

'Mark, are you ready to see Olivia Collins?'

'Of course.' Mark's smile was welcoming. Quite different from the previous flirtatious curve of Jeremy's lips. How could she have been so taken in by Jeremy? The man really was a bit of a sleaze. Had she been desperate enough for attention to accept anything that had come along? If it had gone any further, would she have been sucked in enough to miss what she had discovered with Mark? What a horrible thought. Penelope smiled back at Mark.

'She's in Resus 3.'

'Is that her trace? Let's have a look.' Mark's gaze focused on the sheet of pink graph paper. Jeremy's gaze focused on Penelope until Mark's quiet whistle redirected his attention.

'Look at this! Supraventricular tachycardia of 230 beats per minute.'

'ST depression as well,' Jeremy added. 'In all the chest leads.'

'That's non-specific in a tachycardia like this.' Mark glanced at Penelope. 'We need to slow the rate and do another ECG. I can't pick any obvious delta waves but we've got inverted P-waves in the inferior leads and V1. It looks like an AV nodal re-entry rhythm. Could be Wolff-Parkinson-White syndrome.'

'She'll need an ablation, then.' Jeremy Lane was

sounding very professional but the look that Penelope caught was an open invitation. She looked away hurriedly, hoping desperately that Mark hadn't caught any shadow of Jeremy's glance.

'Do you want me to call someone down from Cardiology?'

'Thanks.' Mark still had the trace in his hand as he moved away from Jeremy. Was it Penelope's imagination or was he looking at the anaesthetist a little too carefully? 'I'll be in with Olivia when you've made the call.'

Jeremy followed Penelope towards the telephone on the sorting desk. 'I need to talk to you, Penny. How 'bout a coffee?'

'I'm busy, Jeremy.' Penelope snatched up the phone. 'I need to speak to the cardiology registrar on duty, please.'

'Later, then.' Jeremy hadn't been put off by her cool tone. 'When are you due for a break?'

Penelope merely shook her head. 'Hello, Anne.' She turned her back slightly on the man beside her. 'Penelope Baker here in Emergency. We've got a fifteen-year-old girl who presented with a syncopal episode. Her 12-lead is showing an SVT of 230. Mark Wallace is querying Wolff-Parkinson-White syndrome.' She listened for a moment, glancing sideways to find Jeremy had finally given up on attracting her attention. He was wandering away with a resigned wave. 'That'll be great, thanks, Anne. She's in Resus 3.'

Penelope replaced the receiver and sighed audibly as she watched Jeremy leave the department. She'd dearly love to be able to wave a wand and make the anaesthetist simply go 'poof' and disappear. The vague disquiet that his continued interest in her generated was the only dark cloud she had on her present horizon. If Jeremy vanished, along with her memory of any attraction to him and the guilt she couldn't quite obliterate concerning her original intentions towards Mark, she would be totally and unbelievably happy.

Far more of her time with Mark was spent in the emergency department of St Margaret's Hospital than anywhere else at present, but the personal interaction that slipped so easily and so privately into their working lives was a pleasure all on its own.

Like the silent laughter that could be shared when dealing with a less than typically serious case. A sixty-five-year-old woman had come in only a couple of nights ago at 2 a.m. The ambulance officer who had handed over the care of their patient to Amanda, the triage nurse, had been having difficulty keeping a straight face himself. The department had been unusually quiet at the time and Mark and Penelope had been sitting at the sorting desk while Amanda listened to the paramedic.

'Myra is having a baby,' the paramedic informed

them. 'Apparently labour started at 8 p.m. last night when her waters broke. The contractions are currently five minutes apart and lasting approximately one minute.'

The woman was lying comfortably on the stretcher in a semi-recumbent position. The blankets covered a plump figure but Myra's abdomen was clearly undistended. Tightly permed grey hair framed a face that an advertising company would have been delighted to have on their books should they have needed an archetypal grandmother. It was a cheerful face and the faded blue eyes behind gold-rimmed spectacles gave no impression of a less than normal state of mind.

'The baby's a breech presentation,' Myra told her new audience, 'otherwise I would have gone for a home delivery. I'm really very sorry to trouble you all at this time of night.'

'That's quite all right.' Mark had joined Amanda who had her lips pressed together too tightly to be able to respond.

'Myra was a midwife,' the paramedic told Mark. 'You'll find she knows exactly what stage of labour she's at.'

'You probably think I'm too old to be having a baby,' Myra suggested to Mark.

'Ah…' Mark made the mistake of catching Penelope's eye. She was very impressed at his facial muscle control but he was unable to suppress the laughter she could see dancing in his eyes. Laughter they would be able to indulge in and share later.

'Especially twins,' Myra continued.

Penelope coughed to cover her own giggle. Amanda was now totally incapable of dealing with the booking in of this case. She excused herself with a despairing roll of her eyes at Penelope before staggering off in the direction of the staffroom. Penelope took the paperwork and began entering details into the computer.

Myra Tottle had no next of kin listed. She lived alone in a retirement village and her marital status had not been checked.

'Mrs Tottle could go into cubicle 4,' Penelope told the ambulance officers.

'It's "Miss" Tottle,' Myra corrected. Her smile was embarrassed. 'Not the done thing, I know, but I don't suppose it matters so much these days and, anyway, I'm sure he'll do the right thing eventually. Don't you think so?'

'It's hard for me to say,' Penelope responded cautiously. She was following the stretcher to cubicle 4. 'What do you think?'

'I think…I think I'm having another contraction! Oh…. Ah-h!' Myra released an ear-piercing shriek. As it faded, Penelope could swear she heard laughter coming from the direction of the staffroom. She sped back towards the sorting desk as the ambulance officers transferred Myra from the stretcher to the bed.

'What on earth are we going to do with her?' she asked Mark desperately.

He was grinning. 'Call in a psych consult. I'm sure they'll enjoy it as much as we will.' He consulted a printout lying on the desk. 'The registrar on duty is David Maitland. I'll have a chat to him if you like.'

'Please. But what am I going to do with Myra in the meantime?'

'Take some vitals. Assess her mental state. Ask her what year she thinks it is and who the prime minister is. The usual stuff.'

'What if she starts screaming again?'

'You could give her some Entonox,' Mark suggested. 'She was a midwife so she'll probably be expecting it.'

'We can't do that!'

'Why not?' Mark was still smiling. 'Just don't turn the cylinder on.' More laughter could be heard from the staffroom. 'I think I might have a quick coffee,' Mark added thoughtfully. 'I can make that call from the staffroom.'

'You'll keep,' Penelope warned. 'I'll expect an appropriate penance for leaving me with this.'

'I'm sure you'll be able to think of something.' Mark's gaze was enough to send a very pleasurable sensation down the length of Penelope's spine. 'Oh, and, Pen?'

'Mmm?'

Mark turned away with a chuckle. 'Don't forget to boil plenty of water.'

Myra stayed in the emergency department for another two hours. The psychiatric registrar, David Maitland, hadn't resented losing his sleep at all. He even stayed, after Myra had been transferred, to have coffee with the other staff.

'Fascinating case,' he said happily. 'She's going to need a thorough physical check. She hasn't got any history of psychiatric illness.'

'Is she schizophrenic?' Mark queried.

'I don't think so,' David responded. 'Schizophrenia seldom develops after the age of forty-five. Elderly people are more likely to be subject to organic ailments with psychiatric manifestations. This is a rather unusual case of delusional disorder.'

'Is she paranoid?'

'Depends how you look at it.' David grinned. 'The father of these twins had been harassing her for a long time, apparently. Myra just found it too hard to defend her virtue in the end.'

'Who does she think the father is?' Penelope asked. 'Another resident at the retirement village?'

'No.' David laughed. 'He comes out of the radio.' He shook his head. 'Bit sad, really. She's spent her life delivering other people's babies and has always wanted one of her own. I think this disorder has been triggered by the move into the village away from long-familiar surroundings.'

'What will you do with her?'

'We'll keep her in for a few days. I've started her on some low-dose antipsychotic medication but she'll need scanning to rule out organic brain disease. I've put her into a general medical ward for now. There could well be some underlying physical problems contributing to this.'

'I hope they've got some Entonox available in the ward,' Mark said with a grin. 'She won't be popular if she screams the place down.'

'I've charted a sedative if it's needed.' David glanced at his watch and then yawned. 'Lord, it's 4 a.m. I think I'll head back to bed and leave you lot here to enjoy yourselves. Have fun.'

Fun seemed to be easy to find when Penelope was on duty at the same time as Mark. Sometimes it was something the whole department could appreciate, like the case of Myra Tottle. At other times the enjoyment was a lot more private. The elderly woman Penelope took charge of later that week wasn't delusional but had a keen sense of humour.

'The hose attacked me,' she told Penelope. 'I swear it was out to get me.'

'It certainly succeeded.' Penelope was having some difficulty in removing the soaked woollen cardigan the woman was wearing. They were in

Resus 2 because of the cardiac arrhythmia discovered when the eighty-year-old had fallen and fractured her wrist after the episode with the garden hose. Mark was examining the wrist.

'It's definitely broken, I'm afraid. We'll send you off for an X-ray as soon as Penny's done your ECG.'

'I only went out to water the pots. I turned the tap on too hard and the end of the hose went crazy.' The woman was shivering. 'I had no intention of getting wet, you know. I feel rather stupid.'

'It's certainly no indication of a lack of intelligence,' Mark observed reassuringly. 'Some people just have a knack of getting wet unintentionally.'

The direct glance at Penelope brought a flush of colour to her cheeks. Was Mark thinking about the cold and wet rescue of the mother and baby from the car accident or was it the day on the beach when that unexpected wave had soaked her? The day when Mark had given her that first kiss?

'The only nice thing about getting wet is being able to take all your clothes off,' their patient observed.

'Hmm.' Mark flashed Penelope the ghost of a wink. 'I'll have to remember that.'

Penelope dropped her gaze, trying to concentrate on placing the electrodes for the ECG. She was only partially successful. The day on the beach seemed a long time ago now. That first kiss had been succeeded by more. Penelope wasn't counting any longer. What was the point in keeping a tally of something she had no intention of stopping? She couldn't imagine ending the accumulation of those kisses now. Not when every one of them seemed to be an improvement on the last.

No wonder she felt so happy. And no wonder that any attention from Jeremy now seemed an inappropriate intrusion. She was living for every moment she and Mark had together. Revelling in every shift they shared, every conversation, every shared coffee or meal. Every date that ended with those bone-melting kisses. Their physical relationship could go no further just yet. Mark's quarters weren't a place Penelope was prepared to sneak into after hours. Not with Jeremy's bedroom just down the hallway. She wasn't about to suggest breaking the firm house rule she and Belinda had about overnight visitors either. Her flat still wouldn't be private enough. The frustration was exciting in a way. They both knew it was only a matter of time and they both knew that if their kisses were any indication, the fulfilment of their raging desire would be more than worth waiting for.

And they wouldn't have to wait much longer. Penelope's next day off on Friday was booked to help Mark shift into the little house above the sea. No house rules there. No undesirable close neighbours. Only the prospect of an old brass bedstead with porcelain flower inserts and a brand-new mattress. Penelope's sigh was one of pure pleasure that stemmed from the anticipation of something she had been waiting for all her adult life. A confirmation that this was the real thing. This was *it*. She had found the person she wanted to spend the rest of her life with.

Friday was a long and tiring day. The furniture arrived by delivery truck early in the morning, with other items such as the refrigerator and washing-machine arriving by separate delivery. Yet another truck brought the personal items Mark had had in storage. Penelope lugged box after box of books into the living area but there were still more waiting in the garage where they were out of the heavy rain. She straightened after depositing a particularly solid load, taking a moment to rub the small of her back.

'Have you got two sets of the Encyclopaedia Britannica or something in these boxes?'

Mark shook his head, grinning. 'Nope. Just lots of good books. I hate parting with anything I've enjoyed reading.'

'Hmm. You must have spent a lot of time reading.'

'Just as well I got those big bookshelves, isn't it?' Mark finished positioning the vast leather couch in front of the fireplace. 'Let's have a coffee,' he suggested.

'We'll have to unpack the kitchen stuff first. I've got no idea where your kettle is.'

'I'll find it.' Mark strode towards the kitchen. 'Oh, no! I forgot to get any milk.'

'Why don't I make a quick trip to a supermarket?' Penelope offered cunningly. 'By the time I get back you'll probably have the kitchen sorted.'

'But I'll need help,' Mark said plaintively. 'Deciding where things should go in a kitchen is...' Dark green eyes glinted mischievously.

'A woman's work?' Penelope finished for him drily. She hid her smile as she picked up her shoulder-bag. 'I'm off,' she announced firmly. 'See if you can rustle up a batch of scones while you're in the kitchen.'

Mark beat her to the door. He positioned himself as a blockade with a hand on each side of the doorframe. Penelope kept moving until her body was in contact with his before glancing up. 'Some whipped cream on those scones would be nice.'

Mark's head dipped and the kiss made Penelope forget completely about her aching back. The familiar ache of desire gained precedence and was heightened considerably by the knowledge that there were no barriers any more. They both had the overwhelming desire and now they had the perfect place to indulge it.

'Um...Pen...?' Mark planted a final soft kiss on her lips.

'Mmm?' Penelope still had her eyes closed.

'Do you think you could pick up a bottle of cream as well as the milk?'

Penelope filled a trolley with supplies from the supermarket. Milk, cream, coffee, tea, bread, bacon, eggs and cereal. She collected fruit and vegetables and anything else she thought Mark might need over the next few days. She smiled as she added flour, butter and jam to the trolley. Maybe she would rustle up a batch of scones herself for lunch.

By the time they did stop for a break it was well past lunchtime. The weather had closed in completely and Penelope was shivering as she returned from yet another trip to the garage.

'It's freezing out there and you should see the surf. I wonder if it ever breaks right onto the road?'

'That'd be good. We'd be cut off from civilisation. Just as well you got so much food.' Mark frowned. 'You really are freezing. And you're *wet*!'

'It's raining.' Penelope grimaced. 'A lot. I couldn't help it.'

'I'll get some wood in,' Mark decided. 'Let's see if this fireplace is as good as it looks.'

It was. The huge fireplace swallowed the dry logs and pumped out enough heat to warm the entire house. Penelope's damp clothes quickly dried out. Daylight faded fast in the abysmal weather conditions but neither Penelope nor Mark minded in the least. They sat on the old leather couch and ate the bacon and egg toasted sandwiches they'd made.

'No scones, then? You could teach me how to make them.'

'Are you kidding? I'm exhausted.' Penelope swapped her plate for the mug of coffee beside her feet.

'Let's stop,' Mark suggested. 'I've got a bottle of champagne in the fridge. I think it's time for our house-warming party.'

'But we've nearly finished unpacking. There's only a few more boxes in the garage. It would be a shame to give up now.'

'OK.' Mark's agreement was reluctant. 'But only for an hour. If we're not done by then I'm blowing the whistle.'

They weren't quite finished an hour later. Mark took the pile of linen from Penelope's arms. 'That's it. Time to stop.'

'But your bed's not made up.'

'I can do that later.'

'You're as tired as I am. You won't want to do it later. Come on, it'll only take two minutes if I help you.'

Mark caught Penelope's determined gaze and sighed. 'You don't give up easily, do you?'

'Nope.' Penelope grinned.

Mark followed her to the bedroom. 'Some people

might even say you were kind of stubborn, Penelope Baker.'

'Only unkind people would say something like that.' Penelope extracted the mattress cover and fitted sheet from the pile in Mark's arms. 'Other people might say I have perseverance and an admirable ability to finish the things that I start.'

Mark smiled as he draped the duvet cover and pillowcases over the brass rail of the bedstead. He caught the end of the sheet on the opposite side of the bed to Penelope's and tucked it over the corner of the mattress. Penelope gathered the duvet inner in her arms and deposited it on top of the bed.

'We'll straighten it out,' she instructed. 'Much easier to get the cover on that way.'

The duvet cover was dark blue with a contrasting cream edging. The pillowcases reversed the combination, being cream with a blue edging. Penelope smoothed a pillow after she'd placed it on the bed.

'Very clever of you to get covers that match the flower inserts so perfectly.' She stepped back. 'It looks great.'

'Pure luck.' Mark was struggling to stuff the other pillow into a case that had somehow turned itself inside out. Penelope moved around the bed.

'Here—let me.' She pulled the pillowcase free and turned it right side out. The pillow slipped inside and she tucked the flap into place. Then she smiled at Mark. 'OK. You're allowed to stop now. Do you still want that champagne?'

'Of course.' Mark was gazing at Penelope steadily. 'But there's something else that I want a lot more.'

Penelope's gaze was firmly caught. She pulled the pillow she was still holding closer to her body. 'What's that?' she asked softly.

Her tone was teasing. She knew what the answer was going to be. She knew what she desperately wanted the answer to be. She also wanted to hear Mark say it.

He obliged. Reaching out with one hand, he pulled the pillow from Penelope's arms and dropped it onto the bed. With his other hand he gently cupped her chin. 'I want you, Penelope Baker.'

His kiss was exquisitely tender. Dark green eyes came into view as Penelope opened her eyes, disappointed by the unexpected interruption to the most perfect kiss she had ever been given.

'I love you, Pen,' Mark told her. 'And I want you. *So* much.'

'I want you, too, Mark,' Penelope whispered. She stroked the dark, wavy hair back from Mark's temples, pulling his face closer as her palms brushed his cheeks. This time the kiss was far from tender. A white-hot passion erupted the second their lips made contact. Later, Penelope could remember little of how they managed to undress each other or move into the bed. It seemed that that kiss never stopped. The touch of those lips, the caress of that tongue, the murmured words or just sounds of desire and, later, fulfilment provided a constant background to love-making that Penelope never wanted to stop. It suspended time but the promise of infinity was tantalisingly brief. It was over far too soon.

'You're unbelievable.' Mark's whisper broke the silence as Penelope lay quietly in his arms. 'How did you do that?'

'Do what?'

'Stop the world turning.' Mark stroked a finger lightly over the curve of Penelope's hip. 'I've never felt anything like that before. Ever.'

Penelope closed her eyes with a soft groan. The touch of that finger was igniting her desire all over again.

'So…how did you do it?' Mark's hand was trailing over her hip towards her thigh now.

'I thought it was you.' Penelope opened her eyes with an effort and then smiled slowly. 'It can't be me. I've never felt anything like that before either.'

'Then it must be us,' Mark said with satisfaction. His lips brushed Penelope's. 'We belong together, Pen.'

'Mmm.' Penelope was wondering how long she might have to wait before they could stop the world turning for a while again. 'I think you might be right.'

'I know I'm right.' Mark raised his head to smile at Penelope. 'Move in with me, Pen. I don't think I ever want to be in this bed by myself.'

Penelope swallowed, too stunned to say anything for several seconds. How had things moved ahead this fast? And how could it feel so right? The silence stretched on as something held Penelope back from saying anything. Something was trying to crowd out the feeling that this was what she wanted, but it took a moment to remember that Greg had wanted her to move in with him as well. It had seemed the logical first step in a permanent relationship, but moving in and sharing a bed had been all that Greg had had in mind and it hadn't lasted. Penelope wanted more than that from Mark. She wasn't about to settle for anything less.

'I can't do that, Mark,' she told him finally.

'Why?' Mark had been watching her carefully. 'We belong together, Pen. You agreed.'

'You want me to share your bed,' Penelope reminded him. 'And that's fine. I want to share it.' She bit her lip shyly. 'As often as possible. But there has to be more to a relationship than that to live together.'

'Of course there does,' Mark agreed. His gaze hadn't left Penelope's face. 'I love you, Pen. It's not just my bed I want you to share. I'm talking about the rest of my life here.'

'You mean...?' The power of speech deserted Penelope.

'I mean that I want you to marry me.' Mark's smile was a little tentative. 'I want you to move in and never leave. My bed *or* my life.'

'Oh, Mark.' Penelope reached out to touch his cheek. 'I don't ever want to leave. I...I love you, too.'

'So, will you? Marry me?'

'Yes. Of course I will.' Penelope found herself pulled very tightly against Mark's body. The joy his proposal had given her was quickly accentuated by the excitement generated by the intimate contact of their bodies. Mark clearly felt the same way. His hand was moving again. His lips were against her ear.

'When?' he whispered.

'Now,' Penelope breathed. 'Please!'

Penelope felt the smile against her ear. 'I meant, when will you marry me?'

'Whenever you like.' Penelope wanted Mark to stop talking. Plans for a wedding could wait. The turning of the world was slowing down and she wanted to stop it completely. Now.

'Don't we need to be engaged for a while first?'

'I suppose so.' Penelope's eyes were firmly shut.

'But not for too long,' Mark persisted. 'We could get married before Christmas.'

'That's only a couple of weeks away!'

'Perfect. We'll get the ring next week and have a really short engagement. Let's get married on Christmas Eve. I rather like the thought that Christmas Day would be the first day of the rest of our lives together.'

'Mmm. Sounds great.' Penelope pushed aside any thought of how difficult it might be for her family members to get flights to attend a wedding during the Christmas holiday rush. There was only one thing she wanted to think about right now. Penelope pressed her hips even closer to Mark, demanding a response. He groaned.

'We'll talk about this later.'

'Mmm,' Penelope repeated. 'Much later.'

CHAPTER SEVEN

'I'VE got vomiting and diarrhoea. *And* a sprained ankle.' Belinda was writing details on the whiteboard near the sorting desk. She wrote 'X-ray' beside the soft tissue injury listed for cubicle 2.

'Poor you.' Penelope grinned at Belinda but she wasn't going to be outdone. 'I've got an intentional overdose and a sore back.' The day had not been filled with challenging patients so far.

'I've got a foreign body in the left eye.'

'Ha! *I've* got a foreign body in the right *nostril*!'

Belinda laughed. 'OK, you win! I can't compete with that. What is it?'

'We think it might be chewing gum. Nobody's been able to delve close enough to find out yet. Haven't you heard the screaming?' Penelope was still smiling broadly as Jack approached the two nurses.

'You're looking far too happy to be working in here.' The senior consultant paused and then grimaced. 'Who's making that dreadful noise?'

'A two-year-old in cubicle 6,' Penelope answered.

'He's got something indeterminate lodged up his right nostril,' Belinda added. The nurses exchanged a glance and giggled.

'Nice to see people so happy in their work.' Jack smiled before casting a thoughtful glance at Penelope. 'Mind you, you've been looking happy for days. Positively glowing, in fact.'

'She's on cloud nine,' Belinda confirmed. 'I'm dead jealous.'

'Am I allowed to know the reason for the current bliss?' Jack was still smiling. 'Or is it just the pleasure of the challenging cases we've been getting lately?'

'Ask Mark Wallace,' Belinda suggested. 'Or wait until tomorrow when you see the ring.'

'*Bindy!*' Penelope's eyes widened in consternation. 'It's supposed to be a *secret*.'

'Everybody knows,' Belinda retaliated.

'I didn't.' Jack looked delighted. 'Congratulations, Penny.'

'Thanks.' Penelope glared at Belinda. 'It was supposed to stay private until we found a ring.'

'You're taking far too long,' Belinda said airily. 'It's been over a week and you know perfectly well that you can't keep a secret in this place.'

'Not with friends like you, that's for sure.'

'It wasn't me that let the cat out of the bag,' Belinda protested. 'More like the fact that Mark was sitting in the staffroom last week with the *Yellow Pages*, making a list of all the addresses of the jewellers' shops in the city.'

Matt joined the small group at the whiteboard.

'Trauma team call,' he announced. 'ETA ten minutes.'

'Excellent!' Belinda's face brightened. 'I'll have to give away my vomiting and diarrhoea.'

'What is it?' Penelope was also delighted to face a potential challenge.

'Multi-system trauma. Car versus tree. Status one. GCS of 3.'

Jack nodded. 'Intubated?'

'No. They've been unable to intubate due to trismus. There's a query basal skull fracture as well so the paramedics haven't used a nasopharyngeal airway either. Oxygen saturation is around eighty-five per cent at present.'

Belinda and Penelope were already on their way to the trauma room. They pulled disposable aprons from the slot in a large box.

'GCS of 3.' Belinda shook her head at Penelope sadly. 'Same as the tree!'

Penelope put on her apron and tied the strings behind herself. The Glasgow coma scale was used to measure a patient's level of consciousness. The highest score in the three categories of eye-opening, verbal and motor responses was fifteen. The lowest score was three and indicated that the patient was totally unresponsive to voice or painful stimuli. A dead person still received a score of one in each category but Penelope had seen many patients, especially young people, come in with a GCS of three,

survive and then go on to make a full recovery. It
was no indication not to perform a full resuscitative
effort.

More staff were gathering as the trauma room was
prepared.

'Who's the airway nurse?' Penelope asked
Belinda as she reached for packs of IV fluids and
tore them open. 'I'm on circulation.'

'It's Amanda today.' Belinda was watching as
staff members donned protective clothing and
started checking equipment. 'I'm team leader.' She
looked away from Penelope. 'Don't forget to check
the batteries on that laryngoscope, Mandy, and have
a good range of ET tubes out. We don't know what
size this patient is yet.'

Penelope unravelled a giving set and removed the
protective cover from the spike. She pushed the
sharp end into the port on the bag of IV fluid and
hung the bag on the hook over the bed. Then she
opened the valve on the tubing to clear the air bub-
bles. Mark was on the other side of the bed, pulling
on a pair of disposable gloves. The smile they exchanged was brief. They both had professional matters to concentrate on. Besides, Jeremy was standing
nearby and Penelope was very aware of the appreciative stare she was receiving from the anaesthetist.
She turned away to lay out supplies on the IV trolley. Thank goodness it was Amanda rather than herself who was the airway nurse in this case. She

would be working far more closely with the other doctors present than with Jeremy.

'ETA four minutes.'

Penelope moved towards the drugs trolley where Matt was drawing medication into syringes. 'Get some atropine, will you, please, Penny? And some more metoclopramide.'

Penelope could still feel Jeremy's gaze as she opened the door of the drug cupboard. At least there was one good aspect about the news of her engagement to Mark spreading through the department. Surely Jeremy would give up his interest in her once he heard the news? She was still drawing up drugs and labelling syringes during the lull that indicated preparations were largely complete in the trauma room. Odd pockets of conversation started as the team waited for the arrival of their patient. Jeremy used the opportunity to stand close to Penelope. Very close.

'Haven't seen you for ages, Penny. Have you been hiding?'

'Not at all.' Penelope twisted the top from a plastic ampoule of metoclopramide and screwed on the syringe.

'You're looking gorgeous.' Jeremy watched her draw up the clear fluid. 'As always.'

Jeremy had an elbow casually resting on the shelf of the trolley. He was leaning towards her, his body language suggesting an intimacy that was disconcerting. Penelope glanced away, hoping nobody else would notice. Especially Mark. To her further consternation Mark was looking directly towards them. Penelope felt her cheeks flush in discomfort as she looked hurriedly away and fumbled for a pen to label the syringe. She didn't want Jeremy's attention but what could she do?

'ETA one minute.'

Staff milled towards the door. Mark walked behind the drugs trolley as Jack arrived, tying on an apron.

'Mark. I believe congratulations are in order. You're a lucky man.'

'Sure am.' Mark's gaze rested on Penelope as he kept moving. She caught her bottom lip between her teeth, hoping that Mark wasn't bothered by the fact that their news was no longer private. He didn't seem upset at all and Penelope returned the smile gratefully.

'Congratulations?' The soft query almost made Penelope jump. She had forgotten that Jeremy was standing so close to her. 'Is there something going on that I haven't heard about?'

Penelope was spared having to answer Jeremy as the outer doors slid open to admit the stretcher and ambulance crew. There was, unfortunately, just enough time to receive the intense stare from Jeremy that announced his ability to put two and two together with no difficulty at all. And that he wasn't pleased by the answer he'd come up with. The icy sensation in the pit of her stomach that the look generated stayed with Penelope even as she focused totally on the job in hand.

The stretcher was being positioned alongside the trauma-room bed.

'This is Sheila Henry. She's forty-two years old.'

The woman was strapped to a backboard and wearing a neck collar. An ambulance officer was holding a bag mask in place, delivering high-concentration oxygen. Three-lead ECG electrodes were in place and a portable cardiac monitor had accompanied the patient. Staff positioned themselves to lift the backboard clear of the stretcher.

'On the count of three.' Mark was the medical team leader. 'One…two…three!'

Belinda was holding the automatic blood-pressure cuff, waiting to attach it to the patient's arm. Penelope picked up shears to help cut the woman's remaining clothing clear.

'This was a high-impact MVA with significant damage to the vehicle on the front and driver's side. Entrapment time was approximately thirty minutes.'

'What was the GCS on arrival?'

'Three. There's a compound fracture of the right tib, fib and ankle. Also an open fracture of the occipital area of the skull.'

'Let's get another wide-bore IV line in. Penny? Fourteen-gauge cannula, thanks.'

It took only seconds for Penelope to arrange the items Mark needed on the bed beside the woman's left arm. Then she picked up the shears again, cutting through the woman's skirt as the straps for the backboard were removed. Matt was at the foot of the bed. He lifted a large dressing and Penelope glimpsed the open fracture of the tibia and fibula. The ankle also had a nasty-looking fracture with the foot at ninety degrees to an exposed ankle joint. Bleeding was minimal, however, and Matt replaced the dressing. Assessment of the patient's orthopaedic injuries would have to wait until her airway, breathing and circulation were stabilised.

Penelope glanced towards the other end of the bed where Amanda Booth had taken over the oxygen supply. Another dressing had been applied to the open fracture at the back of the woman's head and it was already soaked with blood. Penelope's hand brushed Jeremy's as she cut the centre of the underwired bra their patient was wearing. Jeremy moved his stethoscope, pushing Penelope's hand away.

'Breath sounds are equal,' he reported. 'No pneumothorax.'

'Systolic blood pressure was initially 120.' A paramedic was still relaying information to Mark. 'Rose to 145 *en route* with widening pulse pressure. Respiration rate has remained around 40 and the heart rate dropped from 130 to 85.'

Penelope took the information on board. The signs indicated a rising intracranial pressure from the head injury. They needed to secure this patient's airway quickly to allow for scanning to assess and treat the damage, hopefully before too much irreversible brain injury occurred. Belinda had been listening as well.

'Do you want someone down from Neurology?'

'Left pupil is fixed and dilated.' Matt had moved to join Amanda at the head of the bed.

Mark nodded at Belinda. 'Go ahead, Bindy. See how soon we can book a CT scan as well.'

'Can we get this collar off?' Jeremy sounded impatient. 'I'd like to get on with intubating this patient. Where the hell is the suxamethonium?'

Penelope moved quickly to locate the syringes with the drugs needed to paralyse the patient prior to intubation. Jeremy ignored her as she handed over the supplies. Amanda was looking worried.

'Penny, can you stabilise the head while I get this collar off?'

'We need some more saline up, Pen.' Matt was checking the fluid replacement.

'Somebody get this *bloody* collar off,' Jeremy snapped.

Matt raised an eyebrow as he exchanged a glance with Amanda. 'I'll stabilise the head,' he told her. 'You get the collar off and do the cricoid pressure.'

Penelope hung a fresh bag of saline, leaning past

the nurse who was attaching 12-lead ECG electrodes. The patient had been on the table for less than two minutes and the stretcher was only now being moved out of the trauma room. So much happened in such a short space of time. It didn't take much to tip the balance of control into an unpleasant tension. Bad temper on the part of one of the senior staff could certainly do it.

Jeremy had his laryngoscope positioned. 'Eight-millimetre tube,' he requested. 'And a bougie.'

Amanda's eyes widened. 'I've only got stylets on the trolley. You never use bougies.'

'Well, today I want to use one.' Jeremy's tone was icy. Amanda dropped the cervical collar onto the bench and cast a despairing glance towards Penelope.

'I'll find it,' Penelope told her. She reached into a cupboard and withdrew the flexible guide for a tracheal tube. She opened the sterile package without touching its contents and held the packet so that Jeremy could remove it easily. He didn't bother looking at Penelope as he snatched the item.

Other staff were still intent on their own tasks but the slightly subdued atmosphere showed they were all aware of Jeremy's performance at the head of the table. Mark was drawing off bloods for screening but his expression was slightly grim as he cast another glance towards the anaesthetist. The procedure of intubation was almost complete and Penelope wasn't the only person ready to breathe a sigh of relief, but there was more tension in store.

'For crying out loud!' Jeremy had attached a syringe to inflate the internal cuff of the endotracheal tube. He had his stethoscope placed over the larynx. 'This cuff is leaking. Who checked it?'

'I did.' Amanda had gone pale. 'It seemed fine.'

'Well, it isn't fine.' Jeremy sounded absolutely furious. 'It's leaking and we'll have to replace it. Someone hyperventilate this patient before she's totally hypoxic.'

The tube was withdrawn and Matt placed a bag mask over the woman's face, squeezing the bag rapidly to deliver high-concentration oxygen. Amanda looked close to tears and horrified glances were being exchanged between other staff members. Belinda stepped closer to Penelope.

'She did check that tube. I watched her and it did seem fine.'

'He should have double-checked it himself,' Penelope whispered back.

'Let's just hope this one works,' Belinda muttered. 'I don't think any of us can take much more of this. Especially Mandy.'

The replacement tube was positioned rapidly and the patient's airway finally secured. The atmosphere lightened as Jeremy adjusted controls on the ventilating equipment, only to dip again as the anaesthetist stepped back and glared at Amanda.

'I can't say I'm impressed with the level of competence I've seen in here today.'

Jack had clearly had enough of Jeremy's performance. 'We can manage now, thanks, Jeremy. We'll call you if we need you.' He shook his head slightly as Jeremy left the room. 'What's the oxygen saturation level looking like now?'

'Up to ninety-four per cent.' Matt had watched Jeremy leave. He leaned towards Mark. 'He should be a surgeon, not an anaesthetist,' he murmured. 'Definitely has the temperament for it.'

'Hmm.' Mark had been as unimpressed as anyone by the display of ill-temper. He could understand the annoyance of faulty equipment, particularly in a situation that demanded urgency and could be life-threatening, but taking it out on other staff members was unproductive. Poor Amanda looked shell-shocked.

Mark intended to have a word with her to reassure the young nurse as soon as they had finished, but the opportunity was lost as Sheila Henry was transferred to CT scanning. Amanda disappeared, along with the other nursing staff, to deal with a backlog of new arrivals.

Mark was called a short time later to see a sick baby in cubicle 7 that Penelope had been given responsibility for. The baby looked sick. He was sitting on the middle of the bed while Penelope was taking baseline vital-sign measurements but he made no move to reach for his mother when Mark entered the cubicle. The appearance of a stranger would normally have prompted a baby to reach out for the security of familiar arms but this baby didn't even turn its head to look for the woman standing on the other side of the bed.

'This is Ethan Dodd,' Penelope told Mark. 'And this is Ethan's mother, Elizabeth.' She unwound the tiny blood-pressure cuff from the infant's arm and turned to write the figure on a chart.

Mark nodded and smiled at the young woman. She looked to be a fairly young mother, in her early twenties at most.

'Ethan's been unwell with vomiting and diarrhoea for about four days,' Penelope continued. 'He's eaten very little and his fluid intake has dropped off markedly today.'

'He always finishes his bottle,' the mother added. 'When he stopped drinking I thought he might be really sick. I couldn't afford to go to the doctor so I brought him in here.'

Mark was making a visual inspection of his patient before risking upsetting the baby by approaching too closely. Ethan was really sick, clearly dehydrated with pale skin and a sunken fontanelle. He should have been assessed long before this. Severe dehydration could lead to an electrolyte imbalance which could prove fatal. Mark couldn't blame the young mother for delaying her request for medical assistance, however. There were plenty of people who were determined to manage on their own, especially if a trip to the doctor and then added costs of medication were enough to tip a precarious financial situation into disaster. And babies could seem only slightly unwell for quite some time. Serious deterioration often came unexpectedly and with dramatic swiftness. Fortunately, an improvement could be almost as rapid but only if treatment was initiated in time.

'How old is Ethan?'

'Fourteen months.'

'Are his vaccinations up to date?'

Elizabeth nodded. 'He's due for another lot next month.'

'Does he have any medical conditions he's being treated for? Has he ever been in hospital before?'

'No. He's always been fine.'

'Normal pregnancy and birth?'

Elizabeth nodded again. She looked down at her baby. 'It's just us, you know. Me and Ethan. We haven't got anybody else and I do my best.' Her bottom lip trembled. 'I should have taken him to the doctor as soon as he got sick but I didn't know it was this bad.'

'You've done the right thing, bringing Ethan to hospital,' Penelope told her. She took hold of Ethan's hand and jiggled it gently to try and attract his attention. The baby was crying but the sound

lacked any vigour. It was just a miserable grizzle
really and Mark noted that no tears were being pro-
duced, which could be another sign of severe dehydration.

'Let's get the rest of his clothes off,' Mark suggested. 'I need to check Ethan's tummy.' He caught
Penelope's eye. 'Vitals?' he queried.

'Mild pyrexia of 38.2. Tachycardia of 135.
Tachypnoea of 30 and he's hypotensive.'

Mark bent over the baby. 'Hello, there, Ethan,' he
said softly. 'Can I listen to your chest, do you
think?'

Penelope tried to distract the baby, hoping to produce a few seconds' silence so that Mark could assess any respiratory noises. She picked up the battered soft toy dog that had accompanied their small
patient.

'Who's this, Ethan? Is he yours? What sound do
dogs make? Woof, woof?'

The attempt was only partially successful but
Mark removed the disc of his stethoscope from
Ethan's chest. 'Nothing obvious,' he reported, 'but
we'll get a chest X-ray done. Now, let's see what
this tummy feels like.'

With Ethan lying down, Mark made reassuring
noises to the baby and tickled his tummy gently before starting his examination. Ethan actually stopped
crying and smiled at Mark briefly. Penelope smiled,
too. It was unusual for a male doctor to be able to

establish an easy rapport with such young children. She could just imagine how good Mark would be as a father when he had children of his own.

Their children. Penelope felt a wash of excited anticipation. She hoped that Mark wouldn't want to wait for long before starting a family. It would be the perfect way to seal the commitment and permanence of the relationship they were about to make official. Maybe tonight, after the purchase of the ring, they could find an opportunity to discuss the timing of the conception of their first child.

Penelope shut her eyes for a second, trying very hard to focus on the professional task in hand, but it wasn't easy. Maybe they could do something a lot more practical than discussing that conception. She took a deep breath and opened her eyes again. Mark was completing his careful palpation of the baby's abdomen which was slightly tender, judging by the increase in the volume of Ethan's renewed cries.

'I can't detect any masses or peritoneal signs,' Mark told Penelope. 'Skin's very pale, cold and dry, though.' He turned to Ethan's mother. 'I suspect it's viral gastroenteritis,' Mark said. 'The real problem at the moment is that Ethan is very dehydrated. He's lost too much fluid from the vomiting and diarrhoea and hasn't been able to drink enough to replace it.'

'I've tried to get him to drink a lot.' Elizabeth sounded defensive. 'I knew that was important. I've given him lots of juice and I boiled the water I used to make it weak.'

'It's not your fault,' Mark reassured her. 'Drinking fluid isn't enough any more, though. We're going to need to put a line into one of Ethan's veins and give him fluid that way—directly into his circulation.'

'You mean like a drip?'

'Exactly.' Mark turned to Penelope. 'We'll take bloods and electrolytes at the same time as getting the IV line in. We'll do a blood-glucose level then as well.' Mark pulled back the cubicle curtain. 'I'll just go and do the lab requisition forms.'

Ethan vomited as soon as Mark had gone. Elizabeth helped Penelope clean up.

'I didn't bring in any clean clothes for him.' Elizabeth sighed. 'Not even a clean nappy.'

'Don't worry about it,' Penelope told her. 'He's going to be perfectly warm enough and we've got a good supply of disposable nappies here. I'll just go and find one and we can make Ethan a bit more comfortable.'

Mark was at the sorting desk, ticking boxes on a blood-test form for the laboratory as Penelope walked past a minute later, having located a supply of fresh nappies.

'Ethan's still vomiting,' she informed Mark. 'And his nappy is absolutely foul.'

'He's a sick little cookie.' Mark nodded. 'We'll get this IV going now and start some fluids. I've called Paediatrics. They're expecting his admission as soon as we've got the line in.'

They walked back to cubicle 7 together. 'This is turning into a busy day,' Mark commented. 'I'm looking forward to finishing work.'

'So am I,' Penelope responded with feeling. Straight after work they were heading out to find a jeweller's shop that could provide her engagement ring. She glanced at Mark who was smiling a very private smile. His thoughts had followed hers instantly.

'What sort of stone do you fancy?' he murmured. 'A sapphire to match your eyes?'

'Maybe an emerald,' Penelope whispered back. 'To match yours.'

A figure brushed past the couple as they paused, snatching only the briefest of moments for the personal interchange. Jeremy ignored them but then turned to flash Penelope a distinctly unpleasant glance. Mark's eyebrows rose sharply.

'What have you done to deserve that? In fact, what is going on with him today?'

'I don't know,' Penelope said uncomfortably as she deliberately avoided Mark's gaze. She knew precisely what was going on. Jeremy's foul mood had started the second he'd learned of her engagement to Mark. Penelope hoped that Mark's interest in the cause of his colleague's lack of good humour would disappear before he could gain any inkling of the truth. Perhaps she could encourage a reduction of that interest.

'I don't know,' she repeated. 'And I really don't care.'

Mark blinked at her tone but the exchange was forgotten as they entered cubicle 7 again. Penelope gathered the items necessary to start an intravenous line in Ethan while Mark explained to Elizabeth what the procedure would involve.

'We use a needle to get into the vein but then we take it out and leave a soft plastic tube in place. That's attached to the bag of fluid. We can control how fast it goes in and give any other medications Ethan might need through the same tube. That means he won't have to have any more injections.'

'Won't he pull the tube out?'

'We'll put a splint on his arm and bandage everything securely into place. We'll make sure he can't pull it out.'

'Is it going to hurt?'

'Not too much, but he's not going to like it,' Mark responded honestly. 'Would you rather wait outside until we're finished?'

Elizabeth looked relieved but then frowned. 'I should stay with him...shouldn't I?'

'Sometimes it's better not to,' Penelope said. 'That way Ethan won't associate you with an unpleasant procedure and you can come back afterwards and give him a cuddle.'

Elizabeth nodded. 'I don't want to watch,' she admitted. 'If that's really OK.'

'It's fine,' Penelope assured her. 'I'll show you where the waiting room is.'

It took only a minute after settling Elizabeth in the waiting room for Mark to be ready to insert the IV line into Ethan's hand. The tourniquet was in place and Penelope held the baby's arm still as Mark swabbed the back of the small hand and then felt for a vein.

'I'm going to need a 22-gauge needle. Or even a 24. This vein feels about the width of a hair.'

'There should be some 22s in with the 20s. Try the box on the bottom shelf of the trolley—far right.' Penelope let go of Ethan's arm and picked up the wailing baby, taking the opportunity to offer a little comfort until Mark found what he needed.

Mark rummaged through the supplies on the lower shelf of the IV trolley. 'I can't find any.'

'There'll be some in the cupboards of the resus areas. I'll go and find some.' Penelope rocked Ethan, whose wails had subsided into miserable hiccups.

'No. You're doing too good a job right there.' Mark eyed the now quieter baby with relief. He pulled back the curtain. 'I'll be right back.'

Resus 1 was unoccupied. Mark opened the cupboard containing boxes of cannulae and checked the labels for gauge sizes. He could hear the sound of a woman crying quietly on the other side of the curtain. A distressed patient or relative perhaps.

'He wasn't getting at you, Mandy.'

'Of course he was. He said I was totally incompetent.'

Mark blinked in surprise. It wasn't a patient or relative in Resus 2. It was two staff members—Amanda Booth had been the airway nurse on the trauma team today. Mark wasn't surprised she was upset. Jeremy had certainly been in a foul mood and Amanda had appeared to be his target. Mark had been tempted to offer Amanda some sympathetic support himself but had been called away too quickly to deal with Ethan Dodd. Still, it sounded like Belinda was looking after her colleague.

Mark took a handful of size 22 cannulae and swapped the box for the even smaller 24s. He'd take a few of those as well just to be on the safe side and to replenish the IV trolley supplies. He tried not to eavesdrop as Belinda offered Amanda some fairly pithy observations on Jeremy's character before repeating her reassurances.

'You were doing just fine, Mandy. It certainly wasn't anything you did that annoyed him. In fact, I know exactly what put Jeremy into orbit.'

'What?'

'He heard about Penny's engagement to Mark.'

The short silence on the other side of the curtain

indicated astonishment on Amanda's part. It was nothing to the stunned pause on Mark's side of the curtain.

'You mean…?'

'Mmm. Jeremy's been interested in Penny for months. Ever since he arrived at St Maggie's.'

Mark had all the supplies he needed now. He should be heading straight back to cubicle 7. Ethan's IV access and fluid replacement was urgent but Mark found himself unable to move temporarily. Maybe young Ethan's treatment was not quite as urgent as finding out something that had huge implications as far as his own life was concerned.

He knew there had been an atmosphere between Penelope and Jeremy. Penelope had reacted rather strangely only minutes ago when he'd asked if she knew what today's episode had been about. So that's what it was. Penelope had rejected the anaesthetist's advances even before Mark had appeared on the scene, but Jeremy hadn't given up. At least, not until now when he'd heard about the engagement. No wonder he wasn't too happy. Mark felt quite happy about it, however. And Amanda sounded a lot happier as well.

'That explains a lot. It's funny, though—I had no idea anything was going on.'

'Nobody did. He never got around to actually asking her out on a date. He was so slow Penny got sick of waiting so she went out with Mark. It was all part of the plan.'

Mark's fingers tightened around the slim plastic and paper packages in his hand. He could feel the blood draining away from his face. This couldn't be happening to him. Not again. But snippets of memories were intruding. Penelope had arranged that first outing with him when he'd been standing at the bar beside Jeremy. Of course the arrangement had been made for the anaesthetist's benefit. To make him jealous. And there were other things. Mark hadn't forgotten that odd look exchanged between Penelope and Belinda when he'd asked if there was something going on between Penelope and Jeremy. The day of the accident when he'd been about to suture her arm. He'd seen Jeremy hanging around Penelope often enough since then as well. What about the day she'd given him that very strange smile? As though she'd been embarrassed at him noticing her talking to the anaesthetist. There was no denying the way Jeremy had been practically drooling over Penelope only last week either. When she'd stopped to discuss that teenager with the heart problem. It was all adding up into a picture Mark didn't want to confront.

Amanda seemed to share a shadow of his horrified disbelief. 'You mean *Penny* was interested in Jeremy?'

'Amazingly enough,' Belinda confirmed. 'So you

can see why Jeremy's so upset. He's been doing his best to persuade Penny to go out with him ever since she started seeing Mark. Now he thinks he's lost so he's feeling a bit humiliated.'

Mark drew in a deep, slow breath, trying to stop the white-hot fury that lapped at his thoughts. Jeremy *thinks* he's lost? Feeling a bit humiliated? It couldn't begin to compare to how he himself was feeling right now. He had been used. Manipulated by a woman to gain desired attention from another man. Exactly what Joanna had used him for. Who said that history never repeated itself?

'But Penny's *engaged* to Mark now.'

Mark almost snorted aloud. As if that mattered. Joanna had accepted his proposal and ring eagerly enough. It had needed that final step to bring her ex into line and have him rush in to rescue her from making the mistake of marrying the wrong man. Mark's teeth were clenched so hard the muscles in his jaw throbbed painfully. He took another deep breath as he heard Belinda chuckle.

'Things didn't go quite according to plan. Penny found she rather liked Mark and…well, everything changed.'

'So the engagement's real?'

'Of course. Penny's planning—'

Mark didn't wait to hear what Penelope might be planning next. *Rather liked him?* Hell, Penelope deserved an Academy Award for her recent performances. So her friend thought the engagement was real? Maybe Penelope was putting on the same act at home. Well, the truth would come out soon enough. The engagement wasn't real and it never would be. He was going to put an end to this sham as quickly as possible.

Right now, in fact.

CHAPTER EIGHT

'It's not the end of the world, Pen.'

'Yes, it is.' Penelope reached for a handful of tissues and blew her nose vigorously. Surely this would be the last time. She had cried enough tears to sink a ship in the last three hours. She was far too exhausted to be bothered crying any more anyway.

'I'll talk to him.' Belinda took a mouthful of wine from the glass she was holding. 'It's my fault, after all.'

'No, it isn't.' Penelope could feel a new batch of tears forming painfully. 'It would have happened anyway.'

Belinda shook her head sadly. 'Whoever it was who heard me talking to Mandy got hold of the wrong end of the stick. I was just trying to explain why she had caught the flak from Jeremy's foul mood. That it was ironic that it had been a plan to get Jeremy's attention that made you go out with Mark in the first place. But I told her that the plan had been thrown out. That you were really in love with Mark—even that you were planning to go out and buy your ring tonight.' Belinda shoved the box of tissues closer to Penelope. 'It doesn't matter what the reason might have been that got you two together. What matters is that what you have now is real.'

'I tried to tell Mark that. He wouldn't listen.'

Belinda shook her head again. 'He's a fool.'

Penelope stared at her untouched glass of wine. 'He said it didn't make any difference what I said to him now. That I had lied to him. And used him.'

'But you're *engaged!* You were going to buy the ring tonight. For heaven's sake, the wedding was planned for Christmas Eve, wasn't it? That's next *week!*'

Penelope's sigh was heartfelt. The two friends were going over old ground now. The discussion and tears had started as soon as Belinda had arrived home to find Penelope unexpectedly sitting, white-faced and frozen with shock, on the couch, instead of being out on the town choosing an engagement ring. The story had been extracted slowly and painfully and ever since they had gone over and over it. Trying to find an explanation. And a solution. Penelope was in a state of complete despair now. There was no solution.

'He said he knew the way these plans worked. Sometimes you had to look like you were really going to go through with it to get the result you actually wanted. He said he wasn't going to play along any more. Not again.'

'What did he mean?'

'I don't know. He wouldn't say and I was too upset to ask.'

'I think he's been jilted before,' Belinda decided. 'In which case it's brought back some bad memories. Maybe he's just trying to do what he wished he'd done in the past. Only this time he's got it wrong.'

'But he hasn't. Not entirely.'

'You should have denied it when he accused you of accepting a date with him to make Jeremy jealous.'

'I couldn't lie,' Penelope protested. 'But it wasn't a *date*. Not really.' Except that wasn't entirely true either and it was that knowledge that had made Penelope feel guilty enough to render her incapable of convincing Mark that he hadn't stumbled onto the real truth of their relationship. 'Oh, hell.' Penelope groaned. 'What am I going to *do*, Bindy?'

'Talk to Mark,' Belinda said firmly. 'Give him a day or two to cool down and then explain things again.'

'He won't want to listen. He said it's over. He could never believe anything I told him ever again.'

'Then he's a bastard,' Belinda declared. 'All men are bastards. You're better off without him.'

'No, I'm not.' Penelope uncurled her legs from under her with difficulty. She felt as though she had been sitting totally immobilised on the couch for ever. 'This was the biggie, Bindy. I'm never going to get over this. I'm going to bed.'

Belinda nodded. 'Things might not look so bad in the morning. Have a sleep in. At least you don't have to go to work for a couple of days.'

Penelope pushed herself wearily to her feet. 'Great, isn't it?' she agreed drily. 'It'll give me lots of time to think.'

Penelope did little else for her two days off. Hours of sitting, staring into space. Long walks, including the one along the beach at Paraparaumu. Torturing herself with the memory of her furniture-shopping expedition with Mark and the kisses on this beach afterwards. Belinda reported that Mark was grim and uncommunicative at work. Everybody knew that something had happened between Penelope and Mark to upset their plans but nobody had any idea what it was. Belinda wasn't saying anything to anybody. She was never going to open her mouth on a personal matter at work again as long as she lived. She had even tried to approach Mark to ask for a moment's private conversation but he had refused.

'He told me it was none of my damned business,' Belinda reported to Penelope.

'Thanks for trying.' Penelope gave up on her barely touched meal. 'I didn't think it would help.'

'He's really upset.' Belinda looked thoughtful. 'If he didn't love you he wouldn't be. There's still hope.'

'Do you think so?' Penelope had tried to suppress the spark she herself had felt when walking on the beach. Surely something as strong as what she and Mark shared couldn't be obliterated this easily.

'Of course there is. When he sees you back at work he'll change his mind. There's bound to be an opportunity to talk. There *has* to be.'

But there wasn't. Penelope returned to work to find Mark had three days off. It was three days of working on autopilot for Penelope. Even a successful resuscitation from a cardiac arrest in the trauma room wasn't enough to ignite any enthusiasm or satisfaction for her. And some patients brought a less than professional desire to tell them to get lost. Like the appearance of a face she recognised instantly on her first day back. Those strange, pale eyes would have been impossible to forget. The long, lank black hair tied into a ponytail was also a feature she would have remembered with no difficulty. Aaron Jacobs was even wearing the same clothes as he had when he'd come in with the injury to his wrist. The denim jacket looked as though it had still not been near a washing-machine. The young man was sitting on a bed in the corridor. Penelope was forced to pause nearby when posting a blood sample into the vacuum delivery system.

'Hi,' Aaron said. He smiled. 'I'm back again.'

'So you are.' Penelope's response was cool. 'What is it this time?'

'Asthma.' Aaron held up the Ventolin inhaler he was clutching.

Penelope despatched the blood samples. If it was asthma it certainly wasn't very severe. Aaron was breathing quickly and noisily but was clearly having no difficulty speaking and he certainly didn't appear distressed. The movement of his chest indicated that a good level of air was being shifted and Penelope couldn't hear any hint of a wheeze. It was probably hyperventilation. Attention-seeking. And Penelope was in no mood to cater for him. She turned away.

'Hey! What about me?' Aaron called. 'Aren't you going to look after me?'

'Not today. You'll have to wait until somebody else comes, Aaron.' Penelope walked away. 'I'm busy.'

She *was* busy. She was also emotionally exhausted and physically weakened. She was losing weight and knew that the amount of make-up she applied was doing little to disguise the dark circles under her eyes. Nobody was going to tell her how happy she looked now. But nobody wanted to upset her by telling her how miserable she looked either. They tried to cheer her up by drawing her into the Christmas preparations for the department. Streamers and decorations were being discreetly hung around the sorting desk. Amanda was wearing a badge that played 'Jingle Bells' when you pushed Santa's nose. Someone else had brought in a tape

deck which sat on the sorting desk, playing carols
that often clashed with the electronic rendition of
'Jingle Bells'. Matt threatened to stamp on
Amanda's badge if he heard it playing one more
time, but the children that came into the department
loved it.

Penelope felt completely isolated. At least three
days of coping with all the sympathy she was
obliquely receiving was good preparation for dealing with her colleagues when Mark came back on
duty. Surely things couldn't get any worse than they
were already. The moment Penelope arrived at work
the following day and Mark walked past her without
a word or even a glance, she knew things had already got significantly worse.

Penelope's heart had begun racing the instant
she'd spotted Mark. The spark of hope that being
forced to work together might lead to a resolution
had ignited into a flame that his ignoral doused with
agonising swiftness. If she was isolated then so was
Mark. He had put an emotional force field around
himself that was clearly impenetrable. Penelope
could only hope that it wouldn't make professional
interaction with him totally impossible. If she
couldn't work with him, there was no hope of even
hanging on to the job she loved and her world would
disintegrate completely. Penelope waited in dread
for the first case they might have to work on together.

On first impression, four-year-old Harry Phelps didn't appear to be a challenging case. The presenting complaint was a nosebleed and the fact that the child looked thin and pale didn't ring any immediate alarm bells for Penelope. Maybe it was genetic. The boy's mother, Jane Phelps, also appeared thin and pale. Penelope settled the pair in cubicle 5. The nosebleed had dwindled to an occasional dribble and Penelope began her baseline checks without expecting this to be anything more than the kind of automatic performance she was becoming expert at.

'How many sleeps till Santa comes, Harry?' Penelope took hold of the child's wrist gently as she felt for his pulse.

'One,' Harry responded quickly. He glanced at his mother for confirmation and then smiled proudly when she nodded. 'He might be going to bring me a bike this year.'

'Really? That's cool.' Penelope wrote down the figure of 115 on her paperwork. Harry had a tachycardia and his skin felt rather warm. 'I'm going to take your temperature now, Harry. See this? It goes in your ear. That's a funny place to take a temperature, isn't it?'

Harry's face crumpled visibly. 'Will it hurt?'

'Not a bit.' It took only seconds to record a fever of 38.4 degrees centigrade. Penelope turned to Harry's mother. 'Has Harry been unwell at all over the last few days?'

'He's been very tired,' Jane Phelps told her. 'And he keeps complaining that things hurt.'

'What things?'

'Oh, it keeps changing. One day it's his knees and then it's his elbows. Today he had a sore wrist. He's been complaining that various bits hurt for months now. We've been living at the doctor's.' Jane sighed. 'I don't know what's wrong with him.'

'How's he been otherwise?'

'OK, I guess.' Jane leaned closer to her son and ruffled the blond curls. 'We've had a bad run of things over winter. One cold after another and ear infections and bronchitis. Our doctor put him on a course of multivitamins. She thought he was a bit run down, what with all the antibiotics and everything.'

'They're orange,' Harry told Penelope. 'And they look like teddy bears.'

Penelope smiled. 'Do they taste nice?'

Harry's expressive little face twisted into a thoughtful expression. 'No.' Then he grinned at Penelope. 'But I eat them anyway.'

'Good for you.' Penelope returned the grin. Her pleasure was tinged with relief. For the first time in days she felt a connection with a patient and it felt great. Maybe the joy she felt in her work would return and then she would have a solid base on which to stand while she sorted out the rest of her life.

Having taken Harry's blood pressure, counted his respiration rate and made a note of his recent medical history, Penelope excused herself from cubicle 5. 'I'll be back very soon,' she promised. 'The doctor will want to have a look at you, too, Harry.'

'The doctor' turned out to be Mark. Penelope took a deep breath when he entered the cubicle.

'This is Harry Phelps,' she informed Mark. 'He's four years old.'

'Hi, Harry.' Mark pulled a single sterile glove from the box on the wall before sitting on the bed beside the small boy. He had avoided looking directly at Penelope. Harry watched Mark with surprise as the doctor put the wrist of the glove to his mouth and blew air into it.

'Harry's presented with an epistaxis that appears to be under control now.' Penelope was also watching Mark as he deftly knotted the wrist of the inflated glove. 'He's also pyrexic at 38.4 and tachycardic. He's complaining of joint pain that seems to be long standing and he's had a series of upper respiratory tract infections over the last few months.'

Mark had a felt-tip pen in his hand. He was drawing on the glove. The fingers were the crest of a rooster. The thumb made a beak and Mark drew an easily recognisable set of eyes and an impressive wattle. He nodded to acknowledge Penelope's presentation of the case and then grinned at his patient as he held up the glove.

'What's this, Harry?'

'A chicken!' Harry beamed. 'Can I have it?'

'Of course.' Mark handed over the inflated rooster. 'Can I have a quick look at you, Harry?'

'Of course,' the child echoed solemnly. 'Do you want to look at my nose first?'

'OK.' Mark was clearly as taken with the small boy's personality as Penelope had been. 'Then I want to feel your neck and under your arms and in your tummy.'

'Why?'

Mark looked wise. 'It's doctor stuff. Sometimes we can feel lumpy bits that tell us things.' His hands were on Harry's neck now, checking for enlarged lymph nodes. 'I need you to tell me things as well, though, Harry. Like what bits have been sore.'

'My legs.' Harry was bouncing the glove, making the rooster peck the blanket. 'And my arms. And sometimes my tummy. Ouch!' He glanced up at Mark. 'Did you find a lumpy bit?'

'Mmm, kind of.' Mark sounded offhand. 'Can I look inside your mouth, please, Harry?'

Harry opened a small mouth impressively widely. He didn't flinch as Mark pressed carefully on a patch of gum. Penelope chewed the inside of her cheek as she saw the gingival bleeding start easily. Alarm bells were ringing now. Mark knew exactly what he was looking for and things were adding up into a disturbing clinical picture. The examination of Harry was thorough. Jane Phelps watched in silence for more than ten minutes.

'It's just a nosebleed, isn't it?' she finally asked anxiously. 'Nothing serious?'

'I can't say for sure what it is at the moment,' Mark told her, 'but we need to run some more tests. I'm a bit concerned about his general condition. He's running quite a fever and he has lymph-node enlargement.' Mark was still examining Harry's abdomen. His hands looked very large against the boy's tiny body. They also looked exquisitely gentle. Penelope looked away. 'Harry's liver and spleen are also a bit enlarged,' Mark commented quietly. 'Does this hurt you, Harry?'

'Nope. Can I go home now? We're going to get the stuff out of the garage for the Christmas tree today and I get to choose what goes on the top.'

'We need to keep you for a bit longer, Harry. We need to have a look at your blood.'

'You can't see my blood.' Harry gave Mark an apologetic look. 'It's on the inside. Unless I fall over,' he added thoughtfully. 'Or my nose leaks.'

Mark hid his smile. 'We need to take a little bit out,' he explained. 'With a needle.'

Harry's eyes widened. 'But that'll hurt!'

'Only a little bit,' Mark promised. 'Nurse Penny is going to put some cream on your hand and that makes the skin go to sleep. Then we can pop a tiny needle in and borrow a little bit of blood.'

It took nearly an hour for the Emla cream to provide surface anaesthesia. Mark insisted on being
called to take the blood samples himself. Then Harry
was taken to have a chest X-ray. Penelope checked
on another patient while he was away. Leanne
Starling had washed down several dozen paracetamol tablets with a bottle of vodka. The washout had
cleared most of the pills from her stomach but she
was still feeling the after-effects of the unpleasant
procedure and the ethanol overdose.

'Go away,' she told Penelope. 'Leave me alone.'

Penelope was happy to oblige once she had taken
the measurements needed to monitor Leanne's condition. They were still waiting for the psych registrar, David Maitland, to come and evaluate the teenager's mental state and decide whether admission
was advisable. Penelope pulled the curtain closed
around the cubicle again as she left, turning to find
Mark looking directly at her for the first time that
day.

'Is Harry Phelps back from X-Ray yet?'

'I don't think so. I'll check.' The eye contact was
painful but Penelope couldn't break it. 'Is he going
to need admission, do you think?'

Mark's nod was curt. 'I've already contacted
Haematology.'

'Poor Harry. In hospital for Christmas. That's not
much of a present.'

'Acute lymphocytic leukaemia isn't much of a

gift either,' Mark said quietly. 'And I'm probably going to have to be the one to present it.'

'Oh, God,' Penelope whispered. She closed her eyes briefly, partly against the awful knowledge of what lay ahead for that delightful child and his family but mostly against the pain that had come with the recognition of how bad Mark felt about this case. This man genuinely cared about his patient and Penelope wanted, so desperately, to have him care about her as well.

'I guess this isn't going to be a great Christmas for any of us,' Mark added. His tone was cool.

'No.' Penelope looked away, fighting back tears. It was supposed to have been the best Christmas ever. The 25th of December had been going to mark the first full day of the rest of their lives together.

'Hey!'

Penelope's eyes snapped open to find that Mark had moved away. Standing in front of her was Aaron Jacobs.

'I'm back again.' He was staring at Penelope intently.

'So you are.' Penelope instinctively took a step backwards. The feigned asthma attack had been only three days ago. There was definitely something weird about this young man. 'What is it this time, Aaron?'

'I burnt my hand.' Aaron held up his right hand. The crêpe bandage was filthy. Had he saved the one used on his wrist after the hammer injury and never bothered washing it? 'Are you going to look after me today, Penny?'

'Not today,' Penelope said firmly, hoping fervently that the statement would prove truthful. She hadn't checked for any new patient assignments on the whiteboard recently.

'But you're a nurse. You like looking after people.' Aaron moved closer and Penelope took another step backwards. 'You like looking after *me*.'

'There are lots of nurses here, Aaron.' Penelope looked around. 'Who brought you in from the waiting room?'

'Nobody.' Aaron looked pleased with himself. 'I came in all by myself. To find you. Will you look at my hand now?'

'No.' Penelope didn't have the emotional energy to deal with this. Harry Phelps's case on top of having to work closely with Mark was proving too much for her. She needed some time out. Surely she was due for a break? 'Look, Aaron,' she snapped, 'you're not allowed to come in here by yourself. You have to take your turn. We're busy. *I'm* busy. Go back to the waiting room or I'll have to call Security.'

Aaron's face closed. His eyelids almost covered the pale blue eyes. For a second, Penelope felt frightened. What sort of reaction would her warning provoke? To her relief Aaron shrugged and then smiled.

'OK. See you later, Penny.'

Not if she could help it. Penelope watched Aaron walk away back towards the waiting room. He walked straight into the end of a bed being pushed in the opposite direction. Sitting on the bed, looking far too small, was the figure of Harry Phelps. He still held the latex glove rooster clutched in his hands and his face registered dismay at the minor collision with Aaron. The orderly pushing the bed looked irritated and Aaron must have said something less than pleasant as he sidestepped the obstacle. Harry's jaw dropped and the orderly shook his head in disbelief. Aaron moved swiftly and disappeared through the main internal doors.

Jane Phelps had missed the byplay because Mark was coming towards her with a sheaf of results in his hands. Even at a distance Penelope could see that Jane knew the news wasn't going to be good. She moved towards the group still obstructing the main corridor.

'Stay with Harry for a bit, would you, Penny? I'm going to take Jane down to the relatives' room for a chat.'

'Sure.' Penelope tried to smile brightly at Harry. 'Hi, Harry. How was your X-ray?'

'They could see inside me!' Harry's eyes were round with wonder. 'I've got bones!'

Penelope helped manoeuvre the bed back to cubicle 5 and pulled the curtain closed. 'How are you feeling, sweetheart?'

'I'm hot,' Harry told her. 'And my legs hurt.'

Harry did look feverish and tired. Penelope repeated the dose of paracetamol Mark had charted earlier. She washed Harry's face and hands with a cool, damp cloth and suggested that he snuggle down in his bed for a rest. With the adaptability of small children, Harry curled up and was sound asleep within a few minutes.

Penelope could hear that Leanne Starling was awake again. David, the psych registrar, must have arrived and Leanne wasn't going to make his evaluation easy.

'I'm not telling you anything,' Penelope heard her shout. 'Go away. I want my clothes. I'm getting out of this place. It stinks!'

Penelope knew she should go and assist David. Instead, she stayed in cubicle 5, holding the hand of the sick little boy as he slept peacefully through the increasing abuse Leanne was showering on life in general and the emergency department of St Margaret's in particular. Between the girl's unpleasant verbal offerings Penelope could hear the faint strains of a Christmas carol from the tape deck on the sorting desk. The carol was 'Silent Night' and Penelope had to smile at the irony. Life was an astonishing mix of disruption and peace at times. Of

joy and pain. Was it possible, in fact, to have one
without an intimate knowledge of the other side of
the coin?

As if to emphasise the philosophical train of her
thoughts, the curtain of cubicle 5 was pulled back
far enough to admit Jane and Mark. The young
mother had looked pale on her arrival in Emergency.
Now she looked as white as a sheet. Her face ad-
vertised a bewildered fear as she gazed first at her
sleeping son and then back towards the doctor who
had a supporting hand on her arm. Jane was search-
ing Mark's face, perhaps hoping desperately that he
would change his mind. That what he'd just told her
about her son couldn't possibly be true.

Mark's expression conveyed an empathy that cut
Penelope to the bone. She wanted to comfort him
so badly that she found herself standing, without
having noticed the movement of her body. Jane took
her place on the chair, reaching out to stroke her
son's face before burying her own anguish in her
hands. Mark moved past Penelope to stand beside
Jane, and Penelope reached out involuntarily to
touch his arm. She wanted him to know that she
understood how he was feeling. That she was there
for him. And that she cared.

So much.

Mark's gaze caught Penelope's and she felt as
though the emotion she was trying to convey
bounced back at her off a steel door. Mark had

closed the connection between them and there was
no way she was going to be allowed access. The
pain of rejection hit Penelope like a physical blow
and she turned to escape, tears already fogging her
vision. She pulled the curtain shut behind her, stumbled blindly past Leanne's cubicle with no conscious
awareness of the girl's continued shouting and then
bumped heavily into someone coming from the corridor leading to the staffroom.

'Penny! What on earth is the matter?' Strong
hands grasped Penelope's arms and the concern in
the voice was enough to open the flood gates. Tears
poured down her face as she felt herself being es-
corted further down the corridor, out of sight of the
emergency department. The hands on her arms became arms around her body and Penelope was grateful, briefly, for the comfort they conveyed.

'What's happened, Penny? Who's upset you? Is
it Mark Wallace?'

'No.' Penelope tried to stifle her tears. 'There's a
little boy. He's got leukaemia…and it's Christmas
time…and…' And Penelope couldn't begin to con-
fess the deeper reasons for her state. Not to the man
who was currently holding her.

'I know. I understand.'

Penelope pulled back. However much she needed
comfort, Jeremy wasn't the person who should be
providing it. Especially as Penelope's peripheral vision informed her that someone else was coming

from the department and heading towards the staff-room for a break.

'What time do you finish, Penny? Let's have that drink I've been promising you for so long.'

Penelope pushed back harder and Jeremy relinquished his hold. She stepped back to catch her balance, only to obstruct the oncoming figure.

'Excuse me,' Mark said icily. 'I wouldn't like to be interrupting anything here.'

'You're not.' Penelope scrubbed at her face with one hand, the realisation of what the scene must have looked like to Mark hitting her with a nasty jolt. She cast a despairing glance first at Jeremy and then towards Mark. Jeremy was looking smug. Penelope expected Mark to look furious but his expression conveyed an emptiness that left absolutely no hope. Even anger would have been preferable to the finality of that blankness. There was no reaction that could have suggested that Mark gave a damn any more. There was no hope of putting things right now.

Absolutely no hope at all.

Penelope knew she shouldn't be at work any longer today. She wasn't capable of caring for other people. She couldn't even care for herself. She walked past Harry's cubicle and then past Leanne's. The teenager was mercifully quiet for the moment, but what did it matter anyway? Penelope wouldn't have been upset by any abuse directed towards herself. She was too overloaded emotionally to take anything else on board. Even the penetrating wail of an outraged toddler failed to register a response. Neither did the sight of Aaron Jacobs sitting in cubicle 1.

'Hello, Penny.'

The fact that both Mark and Jeremy had followed Penelope back into the department kept her moving. She didn't acknowledge Aaron's greeting. She needed to escape.

'Hey!' The demand for attention was violent enough to cut through every other sound in the busy department. It was intrusive enough to finally penetrate the mental fog and halt Penelope's movement.

'I said hello, Penny!' Aaron's lips were curled into something unlike any smile Penelope had ever seen. He leapt from the bed and grabbed her arm. 'You're going to look after me this time.'

Aaron's voice wasn't nearly as loud as his initial shout but the department had all frozen to watch. The menacing tone had not quite rung alarm bells for anyone but the potential for something significant to occur was palpable. Even the wailing toddler had been surprised into silence and watched the developing scene from its mother's arms near the sorting desk. Two ambulance stretchers waiting with patients to be transferred, were in front of the mother. Medical staff had emerged from resus areas and cubicles to see what was going on. Mark had paused, his hand on the curtain of cubicle 5. Jeremy was beside cubicle 3, from which Leanne had emerged.

The grip on Penelope's arm was vicious. She instinctively pulled, trying to break free, only to find herself dragged closer to the bed in cubicle 1. The duffel bag that lay in the cage for patient belongings under the bed wasn't fastened by its drawstring. Aaron leaned down, pulling Penelope with him.

'You can't tell me to go away this time, Penny.' Aaron sounded satisfied. 'I've made sure you're going to look after me.'

Penelope could see what Aaron was pulling from the duffel bag. She could see its shape and its weight and its danger, yet it took a long moment to believe what she was seeing. Aaron jerked her upright again. Now he had an audience of dozens of people. People immobilised by shock—their faces registering exactly the same stunned disbelief that Penelope was experiencing.

'You lot don't think I'm going to use this, do you?' Aaron was smiling. He even chuckled. 'Well, I've got news for you bastards.'

Penelope's arm was released with a shove that sent her sprawling towards the floor. As she fell she was aware of Aaron using both his hands to raise the sawn-off shotgun. The screams of terror from more than one person in the crowded department were cut short by the overwhelming noise level of a shot being fired.

And then another.

CHAPTER NINE

THE silence was unexpected.

It wasn't complete. A telephone still rang. The alarm indicating a malfunction on a cardiac monitor beeped and the Christmas carol 'Deck the Halls' emanated quietly and incongruously from the tape deck. These sounds were magnified by the sudden discontinuance of any human sounds. The pause lasted only the briefest second but it was memorable because it marked the real transition from normality to nightmare.

Penelope pushed herself up from her sprawled position on the floor. She didn't even attempt to stand up. She crawled in a blind panic on her hands and knees to try and distance herself from the figure beside the bed. The solid side wall of cubicle 1 presented an obstacle she had to turn away from, and as she changed direction she was forced to register everything going on around her.

Aaron hadn't moved. His posture was almost relaxed and his movements appeared slow and deliberate as he cracked open the sawn-off shotgun he was holding and draped the weapon over his left arm. With his right hand he reached into the duffel bag and removed a handful of shells which he dropped onto the top of the bed. He was actually smiling as he selected new ammunition to reload the gun.

Like some form of trick photography, Aaron's calm and deliberate actions were being superimposed on a background of activity that had been sped up by panic to such a degree that Penelope could only absorb fragments of the chaos.

She could see Leanne Starling lying on the floor outside cubicle 3. The curtain of the cubicle was covered in a spray of bloodstains and the dark pool of liquid framing the teenaged girl's head was expanding relentlessly. David, who had also been in cubicle 3, emerged at a run, sidestepping Mark who was moving towards Penelope. Penelope saw David's foot contact the puddle of blood and could see that he was heading for a disastrous fall as he slipped. Mark could do nothing to assist as he was shoved aside by Jeremy who was also trying to flee but in the opposite direction, perhaps towards the safety of the staffroom.

Jeremy's escape route was blocked by others. Jane had Harry in her arms. A nurse was pulling another patient by the hand. The reception desk was being abandoned. Beds were being moved from the resus areas and people pushed past, desperate to escape. The automatic doors to the ambulance bay opened and ambulance officers backed out, taking the first stretcher in the queue. The doors slid shut again, leaving an older gentleman climbing off the other stretcher, reaching towards the woman standing beside him. The mother holding the crying toddler had gone first towards the outside door and then turned as they shut. She ran into a bed being pulled from Resus 2, lost her balance and had to catch hold of the bed to prevent a fall. The toddler pulled away from her, clearly terrified by the panic and noise around him.

The noise level was astonishing after that moment of deadly silence. Telephones were ringing, unanswered. Alarm buttons had been pushed and abandoned monitoring equipment beeped relentlessly. The Christmas carols from the tape deck were now completely drowned by shouting and cries for help. A stainless-steel trolley was overturned somewhere and the impact of it hitting the floor sounded enough like another shot to cause a scream from a patient still trapped in the department.

'*Stay where you are!*' Aaron's yell cut into the chaos like a knife. The gun was now reloaded and pointing into the department again. '*Nobody move!*'

The scene froze again and the fragments of what had been happening continued to tumble through Penelope's brain. People had escaped. A lot of people. But no one was moving now. The window of opportunity had lasted less than a minute and now it was gone. Everybody left in the emergency department was now under the control of Aaron Jacobs. It was a lottery which of them would not survive the next few seconds. Penelope's back was against the cubicle wall. She had been trying to stand but now she slid down into a crouch, immobilised by Aaron's command.

'Do exactly as he says.' The quiet reinforcement of Aaron's instruction came from Mark. He was crouched beside the still form of David. His hand was on the other doctor's neck where he had clearly been checking for a pulse. He was watching Aaron as he spoke, and Penelope cringed. How could Mark draw attention to himself like that? He was inviting Aaron to use him as a target and he was the closest person to the gunman other than herself.

The closest person who was alive, that was. Leanne was obviously dead. Penelope could see that the side of her head had been blown away by the shotgun blast. The teenager lay in a lake of blood, her open eyes staring sightlessly towards her killer. And David? The registrar had fallen very heavily after slipping in the pool of blood. Was he dead or simply unconscious? Jeremy had almost escaped. He'd tried to get into the corridor leading towards the staffroom. The bed that blocked the exit was empty. Had Jeremy helped a patient to safety first?

The elderly man who had been climbing off the ambulance stretcher beside the sorting desk had subsided back into a sitting position against the pillows.

He looked grey and was clutching his chest with one hand. His other hand was being gripped by the terrified woman beside him. She must be his wife, Penelope thought haphazardly. She wondered if the woman knew that her husband was probably having a heart attack. The toddler who had been separated from his mother had crawled to a halt beside the woman's legs. He sat, quietly for now, with his thumb in his mouth, gazing up at the elderly woman. His expression was one of almost comic bewilderment, as though he couldn't understand how his mother's appearance could have changed so dramatically.

Beyond the elderly couple by the desk Penelope could see the legs of someone who lay on the floor amidst bloodstains she hadn't noticed earlier. Two shots had been fired initially. Had they both found targets with instantly fatal results? A crouched figure in uniform could be seen just inside the doors of the trauma room. The eyes of the student nurse, Chrissy, were dark pools of fear in a face that was ghostly pale. Penelope couldn't see anybody else. Were others—perhaps including the child's mother—crouching below the level of the desk? Hiding in fear of their lives?

Strangely, Penelope felt calmer now. Maybe that was because Mark had assumed the mantle of leadership on behalf of this situation's victims. Penelope allowed her gaze to rest on Mark, drawing strength from the fact that they were in this together. She had someone here that she wanted to protect even more than she wanted to protect herself. She knew she would be able to find whatever courage she needed to do that.

Mark was still trying to maintain eye contact with Aaron but the young gunman was turning. Turning his body and his weapon to face Penelope.

'You'll have to look after me now.' The statement was matter-of-fact. 'Even if you don't give a damn.'

'Of course I give a damn, Aaron.' Penelope couldn't believe how normal her voice sounded. She dragged her gaze away from Mark, forcing herself to look directly at Aaron. Forcing herself to meet the intense stare from those disturbing pale eyes. 'I will look after you.' Penelope took a quick breath to steady herself. 'But you're going to have to put that gun down.'

'No way. This…' Aaron jerked the shotgun and Penelope could feel the collective cringe from everybody still within range. 'This is the only way anyone's going to give a damn about what happens to me. I know. You all think I'm a loser. They told me.'

'Who told you that, Aaron?' Mark sounded calm. Interested, even.

'They did.' Aaron answered the query but his gaze was still firmly on Penelope. 'They've been telling me things for years. Ever since my mum walked out.'

'Have they?' Mark still sounded interested. He was clearly trying to divert Aaron's attention from Penelope. 'How old were you when that happened?'

'Eight.'

'Did you still have your dad?'

'Of course I did. And he didn't give a toss about me either. Even when I hurt myself. I had to keep hurting myself more and more until someone took some notice of me. I thought the nurses cared but they were only pretending.' Aaron's eyes narrowed as he glared at Penelope. 'Like you did. You pretended to care when I hurt my wrist with the hammer but you couldn't even be bothered to talk to me the next time I came in.'

Penelope was trying to remember Aaron's second visit. It had only been a few days ago. What had he come in for? That's right—the asthma attack that had really been hyperventilation and attention-seeking. Her first day back at work after trying to come to terms with the emotional trauma of the break-up of her relationship with Mark.

'I'm sorry about that, Aaron,' Penelope told him. 'It was a really bad day for me. I should have tried to help you.'

Penelope was quite sincere in her apology. There was no excuse for letting personal problems undermine professional competency. Her instincts had

warned her that Aaron could be trouble. She'd recognised that the problem might well be psychiatric.
If only she'd followed her instincts and had tried to
do something proactive. But how could she possibly
have known? If they took the time to try and gain
psychiatric evaluation of all their troublesome, attention-seeking, frequent visitors, there would be no
time to care for genuine emergencies.

'You didn't, though, did you?' Aaron snorted de-
risively. 'Nobody does, more than once. I have to
keep finding new people because they only ever care
the first time. Then they get sick of you and can't
be bothered and they want to lock you away so you
can't bother anyone else and they want to give you
pills so you don't know who you are and you won't
care that nobody gives a damn.'

'Sometimes we get busy, Aaron.' She caught a
movement in her peripheral vision. The toddler was
on the move, crawling around the back of the
stretcher. Penelope spoke quickly, hoping to distract
Aaron. 'Sometimes we have to try and decide who
needs to be looked after the most. We don't always
get it right but some people who come into
Emergency might die if we didn't take care of them
first. It doesn't mean we don't care about the others.'

Aaron didn't appear to be listening. 'They told
me about those pills and what they did. So, you
know what I did?' Aaron's eyebrows rose question-
ingly as he paused, clearly expecting a response.

Penelope shook her head hurriedly. 'I hid them. In front of my teeth. See?' He pulled his top lip up to demonstrate. 'Then I could spit them out later when they weren't looking.'

'Who told you about the pills, Aaron?' Mark joined the conversation again and Aaron frowned at the interruption but then responded reluctantly.

'They did.'

'The doctors? The nurses?'

'No.' Aaron was scathing about Mark's lack of comprehension. '*They* did. The ones that *tell* me things.'

'Are they talking to you at the moment?'

Aaron's gaze finally turned away from Penelope but he didn't look at Mark. He appeared to be staring at nothing in particular as he listened for something Penelope knew no one else would be able to hear.

'No,' Aaron decided. He shrugged. 'But they'll tell me when I need to do something. Like they did about the gun. They care about what happens to me. They knew what I had to do to get looked after.'

'But you're not being looked after,' Mark observed casually. 'You've hurt your hand, Aaron. Why don't you let me have a look at it for you? I'm a doctor. I can help you.'

'No.' Aaron's grip on the shotgun tightened as he swung to face Mark. 'Doctors are the worst. They don't even pretend to care. They just tell the nurses what to do. *She's* going to look after my hand. Penny.'

'I can't let her do that.' Mark still sounded calm. 'Not while you're holding that gun.'

Penelope bit her lip hard. Mark was trying to protect her. Putting himself in danger in order to do so. Would he do that for anyone in her position or did he still care? She had no time to register more than a fleeting flash of hope. The few minutes she and Mark had just spent in conversation with Aaron were disrupted by several simultaneous distractions. The change in Aaron's body language at their intrusion signalled the end of any progress in communication they might have been making.

The first distraction was the groan from David as he began to regain consciousness. Still lying beside Mark's feet, the young doctor groaned again and tried to move. Mark laid his hand on David's shoulder.

'Stay still, mate,' he instructed quietly. 'As still as you can for the moment.'

David's groan was echoed almost immediately by a cry of pain from the elderly man on the stretcher. It was enough to make his wife send an anguished plea in Mark's direction.

'You're a doctor, aren't you? Please, can't you help my husband? It's his heart—'

'Shut *up*!' Aaron shouted angrily. His gaze had gone from David to Mark to the elderly couple in rapid sequence and he was starting to look flustered. Penelope knew how dangerous that could prove to be. This was a volatile situation and it wouldn't need much more to prompt Aaron into using that gun again.

The final straw could well have been the toddler whose forward motion had taken him away from the stretcher, past the doors of the trauma room and towards cubicle 1. The angry tone of Aaron's command was enough to frighten the young child who screwed up his face and emitted a piercing cry of distress.

Aaron's focus changed again. The gun was now pointing at the tiny boy. Penelope gasped in horror.

'Don't hurt the baby, Aaron. *Please!*' She threw herself forward and gathered the child into her arms. The toddler howled in fear.

'Shut it *up*,' Aaron screamed. 'I can't think with that noise.'

'Let Penny take the baby away, Aaron.' Mark's voice was reassuring. 'Then it will be much quieter.'

'No.' Aaron's head swung towards Mark. His respiration rate had increased markedly and a sheen of perspiration was evident on his forehead. 'Penny's not going anywhere.'

'I'll go.' The offer came from an unexpected direction. Jeremy had been a part of the silent audience until now. Penelope had almost forgotten he was still present in the department. 'I can look after the kid.' Jeremy was trying unsuccessfully to sound calm. 'I know about kids,' he added nervously. 'I've got three of my own.'

Penelope was startled. Jeremy had *children*? *Three* of them?

Aaron ignored Jeremy. 'You.' The jerk of the shotgun's barrel emphasised his focus on Mark. 'You take the kid. Get it out of here.'

'I'm not going anywhere, Aaron. Let Penny go.'

Penelope held the crying toddler tighter, closing her eyes for a second. Mark was giving up a chance to escape, giving up his own safety. And he was trying to give it to her. Penelope opened her eyes to find Mark's gaze on her and she knew in that instant that this wasn't something he would automatically have done for anyone in this dangerous situation. He was absolutely determined to protect her and that brief eye contact told Penelope why. Mark loved her. *Really* loved her. He was going to do whatever it took to ensure her safety. The message was easily understood because Penelope felt exactly the same way.

'Please, go, Mark.' The quiet words were spoken with an urgency only the two of them could fully appreciate. 'Take the baby and get out of here.'

Mark didn't have time to respond before Aaron moved, but the words would have been redundant. The visual communication may as well have been telepathic. Mark wasn't going anywhere. Not without Penelope. He stood up sharply as Aaron stepped towards Penelope, clearly ready to defend her physically as the child was pulled from her arms. David's determined effort to push himself into a sitting position diverted his attention only fractionally, but it was enough time for Aaron to send the toddler sprawling and for him to grip Penelope's arm and haul her to her feet.

The tiny child picked himself up from the floor and tried to run. He fell after only a few steps, landing beside Chrissy, who was still huddled, terrified, beside the doors to the trauma room.

'Get it out of here. *Now!*' Aaron shouted.

Chrissy needed no further direction. With a strangled sob, she grabbed the child and scrambled to her feet. The desperate glance Penelope received conveyed nothing more than the young nurse's terror before Chrissy turned and stumbled past the elderly couple towards the internal doors to the main hospital wing. The sound of the child's wails receded as the doors opened just enough to let Chrissy through and then closed again decisively.

David was now sitting up, holding his head in his hands. Mark had crouched again. His hand was on David's wrist and his mouth close to his colleague's ear as he spoke too quietly to be overheard.

Now on her feet, her arm gripped with painful force by Aaron and the cold steel of the shotgun barrel only inches away made Penelope focus with

remarkable clarity. She was vividly aware of everything around her. The condition of the elderly man
on the stretcher was serious and deteriorating. His
level of consciousness was dropping and his wife
was crying. David's level of consciousness was rapidly increasing. He was watching Aaron and nod-
ding at something Mark had whispered. Were they
planning some kind of move on Aaron? If so, they
might not get much help from Jeremy, who was
shrinking into the background as much as he could.

Penelope's new position also allowed her a quick
glance through the external doors to a section of the
ambulance bay. She could see an abandoned ambulance, the nose of a police car parked to seal the
area, police dogs being unloaded from the back of
a van and she even caught a glimpse of a black-clad
figure that she recognised as part of the armed offenders squad. The knowledge that expert resources
were massing to deal with this situation gave
Penelope a new feeling of confidence. They would
get through this somehow. All of them. Aaron
hadn't used the gun again yet and he might not if
they could somehow keep a lid on what was happening in the department for long enough.

Memories of a lecture on behavioural psychology
filtered into Penelope's head during her rapid evaluation. She tried to pull the wisps of information
into some semblance of useful order. The overall
impression given had been one of co-operation with

the aggressor. Not to threaten or challenge a psychiatric patient in any way that might tip them over the edge. The means of dealing with the situation was to try and communicate and gain their co-operation. As much privacy as possible was desirable and Penelope knew she needed to stay calm. Not make any quick movements or try and hurry Aaron into any form of action. Penelope could only hope that Aaron had not seen past her to notice what was happening outside.

'Let's go somewhere quiet, Aaron,' she suggested. 'Into the trauma room over there, maybe. There's everything I need to look after your hand in there and nobody else will be able to see us.' More importantly, Aaron wouldn't be able to see outside from the trauma room and it would also leave the whole emergency department available for the positioning of other potential rescuers.

'What's wrong with him?' Aaron was staring at the man on the stretcher. The elderly man's eyes were closed. He was clearly struggling to breathe and his lips were taking on a nasty bluish tinge.

'I think he's having a heart attack,' Penelope responded.

'Why aren't you helping him?' Aaron sounded puzzled. 'You're a nurse. You're supposed to help people. He might die if you don't help. I don't want anyone to die.'

Penelope pushed aside the wave of confusion.

What was going on in Aaron's head? Was he not aware of Leanne's body only a few feet away from where they stood? Or the legs of the other probable victim which hadn't moved even slightly from their obscured position behind the sorting desk. Did Aaron not realise he was responsible? He wasn't very likely to respond to reasoning, but maybe she could take advantage of his changed mood to sort this disaster out.

'I want to help him, Aaron. Will you let me?'

'I'll help, too.' Mark rose to his feet smoothly.

'Do it, then. Both of you. Do it now.' Aaron released the grip he had on Penelope's arm and stepped back. The shotgun was pointing towards the floor now almost as though he had forgotten he was holding it. Mark walked slowly towards Penelope.

'Move quietly,' he advised softly. 'He could change his mind about this any time.'

Penelope and Mark reached the stretcher. The relief in the elderly woman's face was pathetic.

'What's his name?' Mark queried.

'Arthur Greer. I'm his wife, Vera.'

'Does he have a history of cardiac problems?'

'He's had a heart attack before. Last year.'

'Arthur?' Penelope had her face near the man's ear. She shook his shoulder. 'Can you hear me, Arthur?' She got no response. Not even the sound of a breath. 'He's not breathing, Mark.'

'Trauma room,' Mark directed curtly. 'It's got the nearest resus gear.'

Avoidance of any quick movements was forgotten. They pushed the stretcher through the open doors of the trauma room and Penelope pulled the handle at the back of the bed to flatten it. She removed the pillow and positioned Arthur Greer's head to open his airway. As she reached for a bag mask unit to start ventilation, Mark was attaching electrodes from the life pack. Penelope laid her hand on their patient's neck.

'No carotid pulse,' she reported.

Mark was watching the interference on the screen settle into a recognisable pattern. 'He's in ventricular fibrillation,' he stated.

Penelope leaned over and placed her hands on Arthur's chest, beginning compressions as Mark ripped open the package containing the orange defibrillation pads. She paused as Mark applied the pads, using the few seconds to attach the tubing from the bag mask to the overhead oxygen supply. She turned the flow on full and held the mask to Arthur's face, squeezing air into his lungs again as Mark adjusted the controls on the life pack to charge up the paddles.

'Stand clear,' he ordered automatically.

The first shock made no difference to the fatal rhythm Arthur's heart had slipped into. Neither did the second. The third shock was more powerful and the trace on the screen revealed a different pattern. Still far from normal, the bizarre shapes were irregular and slow.

'Draw up some adrenaline, Pen,' Mark instructed. 'And some atropine. I'll get a line in.'

Penelope turned quickly towards the drug cupboard. Her line of vision swept past the doors and her step faltered momentarily. For the tense few minutes of the resuscitation so far she had actually forgotten about Aaron. And the gun. And the dead people lying in the emergency department. Arthur Greer's wife was standing just inside the doors. Jeremy and David were being moved. With the shotgun pointing towards them, Jeremy had an arm supporting David as he walked somewhat unsteadily into the trauma room.

Penelope's hands were shaking as she drew up the drugs Mark had requested.

'Is he alive?' The query from Aaron sounded less than concerned.

'Yes, but he needs more help.'

'Someone else can do it. There's too many people in here. Get rid of him,' Aaron ordered curtly. 'It's my turn now. You can go away as well.' Aaron cast only a brief glance at Vera. Then at Jeremy and David. 'In fact, you can all go away. I only need Penny.'

David took hold of Vera's arm and pushed her gently towards the door. 'Go ahead,' he advised.

'I'll help with the stretcher.' He moved slowly to pick up the handle at Arthur's feet.

Mark stepped away from the head end of the stretcher as Jeremy picked up the other handle. Jeremy was looking at Penelope.

'Sorry,' he said very quietly. 'I'll make sure they get some help in for you soon.'

'Shut up.' Aaron fortunately hadn't heard what Jeremy had said but he clearly disliked the tone. 'And get out. All of you.'

David and Jeremy pushed the stretcher through the doors. Mark remained where he was.

'Get out,' Aaron repeated. He jerked the gun towards Mark.

'I'm not leaving.'

'I'll kill you, then.'

'If you hurt Mark, I won't help you, Aaron.' Penelope forgot about not challenging or threatening a psychotic patient. Was she too exhausted to care or was it that nothing would matter any more if Mark wasn't alive? 'I'll just walk out and leave you alone.'

'You can't!' Aaron changed the direction of the gun barrel. 'I'd kill you as well.'

'Then who would help you? You'd be all by yourself, Aaron.'

Aaron looked from Penelope to Mark and back again, clearly finding the new turn of events difficult to deal with. He shut his eyes, his head began to nod and then his whole body rocked gently.

Penelope stood very still beside Mark. The gun was loaded. It had two shells in it. It would take only a split second for Aaron to open his eyes, aim the weapon and fire at least one shot. There was no way that she and Mark could hope to close the distance and disarm Aaron. What thoughts were going through the disturbed mind of the young gunman right now?

The knowledge that any second now they would find out just how much longer she and Mark might have to be together prompted Penelope to stretch out her hand, seeking comfort from the man beside her. Mark grasped her hand, squeezing her fingers with firm reassurance. He was here, the touch said. They were together and they could face anything.

Aaron stopped the rocking movement of his body. His grip on the shotgun tightened decisively and Penelope's mouth went completely dry. She knew that the finale of this drama was about to start.

Her future hung in the balance and that future could never be what she wanted it to be unless it included Mark. Even if only one of them didn't make it through this, her life would be over.

Aaron's pale eyes snapped open as the telephone in the trauma room began to ring.

CHAPTER TEN

THE telephone continued to ring.

The strident sound appeared to disconcert Aaron. His pale gaze changed direction constantly—from Penelope to Mark to the telephone and then to the open doors of the trauma room through which they could all see the eerily deserted emergency department of St Margaret's Hospital.

'Who's calling?' Aaron snapped. 'What do they want?'

'They might want to talk to you, Aaron,' Mark suggested. 'To make sure you're all right.'

'They don't give a damn about me.' Aaron edged towards the telephone, keeping his gun trained on Penelope and Mark. Still glancing frequently over his shoulder at the open doors, he stretched out one arm as soon as he was within reach of the wall phone. The call wasn't answered. Aaron ripped the appliance free from the wall and hurled it to the floor where it bounced with a jarring crash and then skidded close to Penelope's foot. She flinched and felt Mark's grip on her hand tighten painfully. Aaron was still preoccupied by the open doors. Another telephone began to ring in the deserted main area of the emergency department.

'Shut the doors,' Aaron ordered. 'I'm not talking to anybody.'

Mark gave Penelope's hand a final squeeze before letting go. He moved slowly to close the double doors. The latch clicked into place and the incongruous strains of the Christmas carols were finally muted completely.

'Lock it.'

'There isn't a lock.'

'Shut the other door as well.' Aaron jerked his head to indicate an internal door to Penelope's left. It led to a tiled shower cubicle, just large enough to fit a bed, designed to be used in cases such as chemical burns that needed flushing. Penelope had only ever seen the shower used to wash down large pieces of contaminated equipment such as stretchers. There would be no lock on that door either and Penelope had to dismiss the wild notion of somehow luring Aaron into the small area and locking him in.

Maybe they could drug him. The cupboard was still open, the ampoules and syringes used to treat Arthur Greer lying on the bench in front of the cupboard. If she'd only thought to fill a syringe full of some potent sedative when she'd had the opportunity, surely she and Mark together would have had no difficulty overpowering Aaron.

Mark could probably do it all by himself but he wasn't going to make the attempt because of the weapon Aaron was holding. The gunman had been careful all along to keep a large space between himself and Mark. A large enough space to pre-empt any attempt to overpower him because it would give him quite enough time to fire another shot. Mark wasn't going to try because the shot that could be fired might well be directed at Penelope.

Mark was moving with slow, deliberate steps towards the door to the shower. Penelope saw him scan his surroundings, including a long glance towards the drug cupboard and the door he was approaching. She could almost see the same possibilities she had been considering tumbling through his mind. No doubt he would come to the same conclusions she had. There was no escape.

Not yet.

What Penelope didn't expect was the suddenness of Mark's move. Aaron hadn't expected it either. Mark reached out and grabbed Penelope's wrist, propelling her sharply towards the space behind the open door. The movement was too fast for Aaron to react to. Too fast for Penelope to regain her balance. She fell forward, landing painfully on the tiled floor. Penelope could feel the movement of the door slamming behind her and instinctively rolled out of the way as Mark lunged for the wall. It was too dark to see what he was doing. She heard several loud thumps and then a scraping noise. She could hear Mark breathing heavily and she could hear the shout of outrage from Aaron, now on the other side of the door.

'*Hey!* What the hell is going *on*?'

Another thump, the sound more muted but the force much greater. The door vibrated and Penelope could feel the disturbance in the confined area. She gasped in fear. Aaron was going to break in and he was furious. The balance had been well and truly tipped now. The sensation from the second jarring thump on the door was interrupted as Mark gathered Penelope into his arms.

'It's all right,' he told her. 'He can't get in. I've jammed a backboard under the handle.'

Penelope's eyes were adjusting to the dimness. The only light was coming from a tiny crack under the door. She could see the outline of the backboard, which must have been left in the shower cubicle to dry after being washed down. The wider end of the board was under the doorhandle with its length angled across the width of the shower cubicle and the narrower foot end edged neatly into the angle between the floor and wall on the other side. She knew the plastic boards had steel reinforcing. It certainly looked strong enough to prevent any attempt to force the door.

The vibrations ceased, only to be replaced by the sounds of furious destruction in the trauma room. Trolleys were being overturned and glass was shattering. Object after object was being hurled at the door to the cubicle. Steel rang on steel as something that sounded as large as a trolley bounced off the door. Penelope cowered in Mark's arms.

'It's all right,' he kept saying quietly. 'We're safe. There's no way he can get in. I suspect this door is strong enough to even withstand gunfire.'

Mark's prediction appeared to be confirmed only seconds later. Surely the crack of sound and the force of that assault on the door could only have come from a shot being fired at close range. The sound echoed around the tiled cell and Penelope couldn't stifle her sob of terror. A second explosion of sound occurred but didn't touch the door. Penelope swallowed painfully. How long would it take Aaron to reload the gun? Mark was stroking her hair. His lips were against her temple.

'It's all right,' he said yet again. 'I'm not going to let anything happen to you, Pen. I'm here. I'm not leaving you. I'll never leave you.'

Penelope listened to Mark's words. She could hear them clearly, partly due to the proximity of his mouth to her ear and partly due to the silence that had fallen on the other side of the door.

'It's gone quiet,' she whispered. 'What's he doing, do you think?'

'No idea.' Mark was listening carefully. 'I can't hear any movement at all.'

'Maybe he's gone.'

'I doubt it. If he stepped out of the trauma room

it would be over in seconds, I would think. The place must be crawling with police by now, just waiting for the opportunity. They haven't been able to take him in here because they can't see what's going on and they won't want to risk injury to us.'

'They won't know it's safe to come in now.'

'No.' Mark's arms gave Penelope a reassuring squeeze. 'But we're safe. All we have to do now is wait it out. He can't hurt anybody else. This *has* to end soon.'

Penelope barely registered the discomfort of sitting on the cold, tiled floor of the cubicle. She sat in the corner, encircled by Mark's arms, the exhaustion of prolonged terror kicking in. The silent minutes ticked on. Or were they only seconds? The impression of time passing was as difficult to gauge as the reality of what they were experiencing.

Penelope's head rested on Mark's shoulder. The feeling of unreality was becoming stronger and her mind wanted to escape trying to deal with it. Her focus closed in so that she was aware only of the man holding her. She listened to his quiet breathing, felt the strong beating of his heart beneath her cheek and she clung to the comfort his touch was providing. She thought of nothing else, until the continuing silence was broken by Mark's quiet voice.

'I'm sorry, Pen. It's my fault all this has happened.'

'That's ridiculous.' Penelope's mind was refreshed enough to concentrate quickly. 'If it's any-body's fault, it's mine. I had my suspicions that Aaron had major psychiatric problems. I could have tried to do something about it the last time he came in with a fake asthma attack. Instead, I goaded him by ignoring him. I knew he was angry and I didn't care. I let my personal life interfere with my job and I knew it was happening. I was just too miserable to care.'

'When was this?'

'A few days ago.'

'Were you miserable because I'd broken our en-gagement?'

'I've never been so miserable in my life.'

'Neither have I.' Mark sighed heavily. 'And it's my fault.'

'No.' Penelope shook her head slowly. 'It was my fault. I wasn't honest enough. You asked me ages ago if anything was going on between me and Jeremy and I said no. It seemed true enough at the time because there wasn't anything going on, but I wanted there to be. At least, I *thought* I did. I knew how wrong I'd been as soon as I got to know you even a little bit. By the time we'd spent that after-noon together I knew that I wasn't remotely inter-ested in Jeremy any more.'

'I knew that, too,' Mark admitted. 'Deep down. I just wasn't prepared to trust my instincts. And I should have been more honest with you. I told you

I left England because things didn't work out. I let
you think it was because of my career prospects but
it had very little to do with that really. I was engaged, Pen. Very briefly engaged—to a woman
called Joanna. I thought I loved her. I thought *she*
loved *me*.'

Mark paused for a long moment and Penelope
waited quietly. She needed to hear this even if it
was hard for Mark to tell her. If she knew there was
a genuine reason for him mistrusting her so much
then it would be much easier to forgive him for putting her through the hell of the last few days. Not
that any of it mattered much any more after the or-
deal they had just been through, and that wasn't
even over yet. Funny how that didn't seem to matter
right now either. Penelope didn't even try to listen
to see whether anything was happening on the other
side of the door. All she wanted to do at that moment was listen to what Mark had to tell her.

'Joanna rang me a few days after we'd bought the
ring and things had been officially announced,'
Mark said. 'She told me that the engagement was
off. She was with her ex-boyfriend and they were
going to be staying together. In the end she admitted
that she'd had no real intention of marrying me.
She'd just wanted to scare her ex into making sure
he didn't lose her. It had been a calculated plan that
she had taken just as far as she needed to. She was

sorry, she said, but I should remember that all was fair in love and war.' Mark sighed heavily.

'How could I not remember? I think it was the most humiliating experience of my life. The man she really wanted was another doctor at the same hospital and you know how fast a juicy piece of gossip like that travels around a hospital grapevine. Everyone felt terribly sorry for me and that made it so much worse. I left because I wanted to forget. I didn't tell you because I thought I'd put it all behind me. Or maybe I've always felt ashamed about it. I hadn't been good enough for Joanna and maybe I thought you might wonder if there was a good reason for that.'

'Hardly!' Penelope smiled, then bit her lip. 'I felt ashamed of even having been interested in Jeremy,' she confessed. 'I suppose I was flattered by his interest in me. It had been a long time since anyone had seemed attracted to me.'

'I find that rather hard to believe.' The touch of Penelope's cheek from Mark's fingers was gentle enough to be poignant. 'You're a stunning woman, Penelope Baker.'

Penelope gave a tiny shake of her head. 'I don't even like him. I can't believe I didn't know he had children. He's probably got a wife as well.'

'He has. He told me she's bringing the kids over from Australia to join him as soon as he's found somewhere for them to live.'

'I feel sorry for his wife. I wonder if she knows how he behaves with other women.'

'Maybe he behaves himself when she's around. From what he's said, I think he cares about her. He certainly cares about his children.'

Penelope's head shake was more obvious this time. 'I don't think Jeremy cares much about anybody other than himself. He couldn't wait to escape out there. He wasn't about to try and help anybody else.'

'He was scared. We all were.'

'You had the chance to escape. You gave it up. You tried to give it to me and when that didn't work you still wouldn't leave.'

'I couldn't.'

'Why not? I wanted you to. I wanted you to be safe.'

'I couldn't leave you behind. There's absolutely no point being safe if you're not with me. My life would mean nothing to me any more without you in it, Pen. I love you too much.'

'It could never be *too* much.' Penelope smiled. 'Not when it's the same way I feel about you.'

'Let's make a pact,' Mark suggested.

Penelope's smile broadened. 'We're good at pacts. See? I'm not wet.'

Mark returned the smile. 'This is a new one. Let's always be completely honest with each other. Even about things we're not proud of. Or things that don't seem important. And let's trust our instincts... because mine are telling me that nothing could destroy the love we have for each other.'

'Mine are, too.' Penelope touched Mark's cheek. 'Don't you think we'd better seal this pact?'

Mark's head bent towards her. 'Consider it sealed, my love.'

The kiss was enough to stop the world turning for at least a couple of minutes. Enough to actually make them both forget that they were sitting trapped in a shower cubicle with someone who wanted to kill them only a few feet away. The absolute silence on the other side of the steel door must have contributed to the way they had been able to distract themselves. As had the confined, dark position and the intimate conversation that seemed to have covered an extraordinary amount of ground.

'It's been quiet for an awfully long time,' Penelope observed. 'Maybe it would be safe to have a look.'

'No. We'll wait.' Mark planted another soft kiss on Penelope's lips. 'I'm not in any hurry to escape any more.'

Penelope grinned. 'You'll never escape from me.'

'I never want to.'

'It would be nice to get out of the shower, though,' Penelope said. Her head pulled back from Mark's approaching kiss swiftly. 'What was that?'

The sounds of movement outside the door brought

a final flash of fear. Mark's arms tightened around her. The knock on the door made them both draw a sharp inward breath.

'Anyone in there? It's the police. It's safe to come out.'

Penelope and Mark scrambled to their feet. As Penelope reached out to support herself on the wall her hands gripped the first projection they found. The shower came on full strength and water poured over her. Mark dropped the backboard he'd moved away from the doorhandle and went to push the shower lever closed, but it was too late. Penelope was drenched.

Bright light flooded into the cubicle as the door to the trauma room opened. Penelope blinked and then blinked again as she tried to clear the water still streaming into her eyes from her saturated hair.

'You're safe now.' The black-clad figure was a member of the armed offenders squad. 'Are either of you injured at all?'

'No. We're fine.' Penelope could see other figures moving behind him amongst the chaos of the trauma room. A police dog nosed an array of destroyed equipment and scattered supplies.

'Where's Aaron?' Mark demanded.

'Over there. He's dead. Looks like he's shot himself.'

People were leading Mark and Penelope away from the scene. Penelope had to look back. Had to see for herself that the threat from Aaron Jacobs was really gone. The sight of the crumpled figure confirmed that Aaron would be no danger to anyone ever again. Penelope clung to Mark's hand as they were led through the emergency department. She didn't look back to where Leanne still lay. Or to see where the other unknown casualty of that initial attack had been taken. She wasn't ready to deal with that just yet. There would be plenty of time to go over what had happened and come to terms with it all. Right now, what mattered most was that she and Mark were safe. And together. And they would always be together.

CHAPTER ELEVEN

It was late.

At midnight the cathedral bells would begin to toll to mark the beginning of Christmas Day.

The bells would unknowingly mark another beginning—that of the shared future of Mark Wallace and Penelope Baker.

The couple stood, hand in hand, just inside the main entrance of Wellington's St Margaret's Hospital. Around them, a group of red-cloaked figures were lighting candles. The small choir was preparing for a midnight carol service in the hospital chapel.

'It's late, isn't it?'

Mark checked his watch. 'Almost 11 p.m.'

'I can't believe how long we've been here.'

'They needed to be thorough. Our statements were important.'

'I didn't want to spend all that time with the counsellor in that debriefing bit. I'd rather we'd had the time just to talk it over by ourselves.'

Mark pulled Penelope gently into his arms. 'We're going to have all the time in the world now. Do you want to go somewhere and talk?'

Penelope shook her head wearily. 'I'm talked out.'

'How are you feeling?'

'Lucky to be alive,' Penelope said quietly. 'And thankful that more people weren't hurt. I really thought that two people had been killed at the beginning but it was only poor Leanne Starling.'

'I don't think I could have played possum as well as that other chap did. Not with a gunshot wound in my arm.'

'I was so pleased to hear he was all right. And Arthur Greer survived as well. The coronary care unit says he's doing well.'

'And David is fine. He's just got a mild concussion.' Mark turned to glance through the main doors as an ambulance drove past. 'The emergency department has finally been cleared. It'll be up and running again in no time, as though nothing terrible had happened.'

'It wasn't all terrible,' Penelope said thoughtfully. She reached up to touch Mark's face. 'It brought us back together.'

Mark dipped his head to place a soft kiss on Penelope's lips. 'It's Christmas Eve,' he reminded her.

'I know.' Penelope nodded towards the choir members who were forming into lines ready to proceed to the chapel. 'Shall we go to the carol service?'

'I don't think so.' Mark smiled. 'The shops are open late tonight. Until midnight.'

'I don't need a Christmas present.' It was Penelope's turn to kiss Mark. 'I've got you.'

'I was thinking of buying something else.'

'What?'

'A ring. Two rings, even. Maybe we can't get married today like we planned but we could buy the rings. We could make a pact to get married as soon as possible.'

'Pacts are good.' Penelope smiled.

'Only when you keep them.' Mark looked stern. 'You got wet. *Again!*'

'I didn't mean to.' Penelope looked down at the scrub suit she was wearing and grinned. 'But I don't think I'm really dressed to go shopping.'

Mark's smile was as tender as the gaze meeting Penelope's. 'You look gorgeous. So gorgeous I don't think I want to go shopping after all. I want to take you home...with me.'

'That's just where I want to be.' Penelope closed her eyes. What she needed most right now was time alone with Mark. Time to affirm their love and the promise of their future together. It would be all she needed to wipe out the aftermath of the trauma they had both survived. Not just the trauma Aaron Jacobs had put them through. Penelope wanted to put the ghost of her broken engagement to rest as well. She opened her eyes again.

'We don't need to rush buying our rings or getting married,' she told Mark seriously. 'We've got all the time in the world now.' A smile teased her lips. 'We don't want to escape, remember?'

'I remember.' Dark green eyes told Penelope that Mark would never forget. 'No escape needed. Ever.'

**Coming in December 2003
to Silhouette Books**

THE
BILLIONAIRE
DRIFTER

by

BEVERLY
BIRD

Disguised as a beach bum, billionaire Max Strong
wants to hide from the glitz and glamour of his
life—until he meets a beautiful stranger who
seduces him and then mysteriously disappears....

**Look for more titles in this exhilarating new series,
available only from Silhouette Books.**

**Five extraordinary siblings.
One dangerous past.
Unlimited potential.**

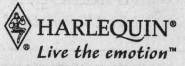

Forrester Square

LEGACIES . LIES . LOVE .

**This brand-new *Forrester Square* story
promises passion, glamour
and riveting secrets!**

Coming in January…

WORD OF HONOR

by

bestselling Harlequin Intrigue® author

DANI SINCLAIR

Hannah Richards is shocked to discover that
the son she gave up at birth is now living with
his natural father, Jack McKay. Ten years ago
Jack had not exactly been father material—
now he was raising their son.
Was a family reunion in their future?

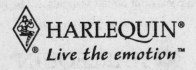

HARLEQUIN®
Live the emotion™

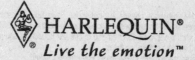

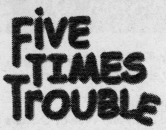
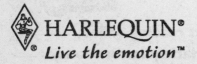